Benedikte Naubert

Herman of Unna

A series of adventures of the fifteenth century. Vol. 2

Benedikte Naubert

Herman of Unna
A series of adventures of the fifteenth century. Vol. 2

ISBN/EAN: 9783337393182

Printed in Europe, USA, Canada, Australia, Japan

Cover: Foto ©Andreas Hilbeck / pixelio.de

More available books at **www.hansebooks.com**

HERMAN of UNNA:

A

SERIES OF ADVENTURES

OF THE

FIFTEENTH CENTURY,

IN WHICH THE

PROCEEDINGS OF THE SECRET TRIBUNAL UNDER
THE EMPERORS WINCESLAUS AND SIGISMOND,
ARE DELINEATED.

———

IN THREE VOLUMES.

———

WRITTEN IN GERMAN

BY PROFESSOR KRAMER.

———

THE SECOND EDITION.

———

VOLUME II.

———

L O N D O N:

Printed for G. G. and J. Robinson, Pater-noster Row.

M D CXC IV.

HERMAN of UNNA.

A

Series of Adventures of the Fifteenth Century, &c.

CHAPTER I.

BY degrees Ida recovered from her swoon. Day had begun to appear. The adventures of the preceding night seemed a dream to her. She looked round and found herself under the portico of St. Bartholomew's. She raised herself upon her knees, and would have gotten upon her feet; but she was unable. In one of the four streets a man approached, whom she perceived to be Walter. She stretched out her arms and called to him as loudly as her strength would permit. He hastened to her assistance. " Come." said he, " let me conduct

Vol. II.   B

" you to your convent. But I had almost
" forgotten to ask, what has brought you
" hither?"—" Alas! do you not then re-
" member," said Ida, whose recollection
now began to return, " do you not remem-
" ber the events that have just passed; for
" surely you were present as well as myself?"

" Talk not to me thus incoherently.
" Ask not such useless questions:" replied
Walter, with some displeasure. " Let us
" begone before any one sees us here."

" Heavens!" exclaimed Ida, " what
" will become of me? Oh, tell me what I
" am to do! you know my unhappy situa-
" tion; you know that my last hopes are
" now annihilated."

Walter was silent, and meditated for
some time how he should act. But he
knew, that, to perform his part with fidelity, he must pretend not to understand her.

Ida besought him to have pity on her,
and to be her friend: " adding, " you can
" best advise me, for you will never con-
" vince me that you are not acquainted

" with every circumstance that has taken ": place." At this Walter grew impatient. She appealed to the deficiency of his left hand, as a proof that he was her conductor. He to his dress, which bore no resemblance to that worn by the man in the mask. Ida having far greater subjects of disquietude, was at length silent, and they arrived at the convent.

Fain would I draw a charitable veil over the manner in which the young Munster was received by the Ursulines, who expected not to see her otherwise than honourably acquitted. At first they were offended that the tribunal had not more favourably treated a person, to whom they had paid such distinguished marks of respect. By degrees, however, doubts crept into their mind; and they began to ask one another, whether Ida were really as innocent as they had supposed her. From that moment she experienced neglect; they endeavoured not to console her, they went not to converse with her in solitude, and soon things were carried so far, that old Walter, who daily visited the parlour, was her only resource.

Ida was at a loss what to think. She felt how alarming was her situation; and yet were her thoughts still more occupied by the stranger who had appeared before the tribunal in her defence.

" Do you not suspect," said she to Walter, " that it was my father?"—Walter shook his head.—" Who was it then? who " could it be?"—" I know not."—O Walter! " I conjure you tell me. You know: " I am sure you do."—" Do you wish, by " talking thus, to drive me from you?"— " Oh! no: but promise me, at least, that " you will befriend my generous, my un- " fortunate defender; and that you will seek " to discover what is become of my father." " Your father! do you know then who " your father is?" Ida looked at him with astonishment, and repeated her demand : and Walter, perceiving that she had not attended to what the stanger had said respecting her birth, but still believed herself the daughter of Munster, again relapsed into his mysterious taciturnity.

Ida began to weep, reproaching the old man with cruelty. Drawn by this charge from his silence, he begged her to be calm, and of good courage, as it was probable her fate would soon undergo a change.

"See my prediction accomplished!" said he to her one morning that he came earlier than usual to visit her.

Ida had already seen too many placards of the secret tribunal, not to know, at the first glance, that the paper he held in his hand was one; but, notwithstanding the agreeable manner in which it was present-, ed, she feared to peruse it, and Walter was obliged to read it to her. It contained . . . imagine, dear reader, the transport of Ida . . . . it contained a solemn declaration of her innocence, and a general acquittal from every charge exhibited against her. Joy now produced on her the effect she had so often experienced from grief. Recovered from her fainting, she a thousand times

B 3

asked if it were indeed true; if they were not deceiving her.—The happy news soon spread, and immediately she was surrounded by nuns, who loaded her with compliments, assurances of friendship, and entreaties never to quit the convent, but to spend the remainder of her life in their tranquil abode.   Ida had not forgotten that the day before she had been given to understand, that, as her innocence was not acknowledged, her residence in the convent could not be of long duration; but she was too happy to think of resenting it. She replied therefore to their civilities with her wonted good-nature, though she was resolved instantly to quit a house, the inhabitants of which could pass so easily from one extreme to the other.

At this moment she was informed that there was a coach at the gate of the convent, which had orders to convey her to the house of count Wirtemberg.

It was natural for Ida to suppose, that, her justification being known, the former friendship of those who had abandoned her in her misfortune would revive; and it was highly pleasing to her to find that the count of Wirtemberg, who had always treated her with marks of attachment, was one of the first to think of her on this occasion. She hastened therefore to the coach, and amused her fancy on the way with a thousand agreeable reveries. She hoped to find, at Wirtemberg's house, her father and her unknown defender, and to be reftored by the count to the favour of the empress. She hoped a thousand things beside: for what indeed will not young persons hope, who are prone to consider the slightest smile of fortune as an infallible earnest of the most signal favours?

Every thing seemed to indicate that Ida would not be wholly deceived in her expectations. She saw the old count of Wirtemberg hasten to meet her, and clasp her in his arms, with an ardour, that would have appeared strange, if in her present situation she had had time to reflect. The

B 4

count led her to his closet, through a crowd
of courtiers, who bowed to the ground to
salute her as she passed.   Having shut the
door : " Ida, my dear Ida !" cried he pressing her in his arms, " my heart did not
" deceive me !"

The timidity of our heroine was alarmed at these lively testimonies of affection ;
and disengaging herself from his embrace,
she fell on her knees before him.

" My lord," said she, " the flattering
" reception with which you honour me, the
" goodness with which you condescend to
" interest yourself in my happiness, lead
" me to believe that you will not refuse to
" carry it one degree farther, that my hap-
" piness may be complete.   I wish, my
" lord, to see my deliverer, that I may
" thank him : I wish also to see my father
" whom I have loft.   The first I imagine
" can be at no great distance, and to find
" the latter will be no difficult task to a
" prince so powerful as you."

" Thy deliverer ! thy father !" replied
the count ; " behold them both in the same

" person."—Ida looked round and perceived herself alone with the count, who pressed her again to his bosom. She looked at him with surprise, and dared not return his caresses.—" Thou does not believe " me! thy heart speaks not for me! I am " thy father. Behold this ornament, which " has discovered to me the secret of thy " birth."

Ida perceived in the hands of the count the chain she had formerly given to Herman; and the recollection of her lover served ftill more to confound her ideas respecting things which were not, to her, easily comprehensible.

The count took pity on her embarrassment. " You still have doubts," cried he : " I must convince you." And ringing a bell, the door opened, and Munster entered.

Neither Munster nor the count had time to utter a syllable; for she instantly ran to throw herself in the arms of the venerable old man, exclaiming : " O my

B 5

" father! do I indeed see you again?"—
" No, madam," answered Munster, taking,
her by the hand, and leading her to the
count, who was at the other end of the
apartment, and whose looks expressed dissatisfaction: No, madam, that honour is too
" great for me; you are the daughter of
" this prince. I was only your foster-fa-
" ther, or rather, to speak the truth, a ra-
" visher, a robber. Behold, my lord," continued he, placing the left hand of Ida into
the right hand of the count, " a new testi-
" mony of the truth of what I have told
" you. This hand still bears the mark be-
" stowed on her when she first saw the light,
" and the ring also which you see cannot
" fail to call to your remembrance that
" amiable consort, to whom the birth of
" your daughter cost her life."—" Ah! I
" need no other proofs," replied the count,
" than the proofs I feel in my heart, and
" those features, so perfectly resembling her
" mother's, that I cannot conceive how I
" have so long been blind to them. Yet

" certain it is, that I have ever been drawn
" towards her by an irresistable sympathy.
" You know, my child, the emotions that
" were excited in me when I first heard
" your name, and the preference with
" which I have distinguished you from
" your companions, in spite of your ene-
" mies."

Joy succeeded to the astonishment of
Ida. Presently she saw herself drawn irre-
sistably towards count Everard; she fell on
his neck, round which she threw one arm,
while she held out the other to Munster,
who wss still too dear for any one to claim
precedence to him in her heart. When the
first transports were over, Ida requested an
explanation of this mystery, which the
reader perhaps is equally impatient to learn.
But how can it be given satisfactorily amidst
the tumult of a thousand different passions?
We will chuse therefore, with thy leave,
dear reader, some calmer moment to impart to thee the various circumstances of so
complicated an event.

Ida perceived with regret, that Munster was far less esteemed by the count than by herself. The count regarded him as a robber who had stolen from him his child; Ida as her guardian, her faithful counsellor, her protector, when abandoned by all the world beside. Count Everard was jealous of the caresses she bestowed on him; while Ida could not forget that she had so long called him by the endearing name of father. A strange circumstance! it must be confessed; and sure I am that many of my readers will be at a loss to comprehend how the pleasure of finding herself the daughter of a prince could fail to obliterate in her every other sentiment.

Still there remained in the breast of our heroine one desire unsatisfied, and which prevented her from fully enjoying the testimonies she received of paternal affection. She had often enquired after her defender, and shown an eagerness to see him, calling him her saviour, and expressing towards him the warmest gratitude; and as often had the count assured her that she owed her safety solely to himself. This indeed she believed from the proofs that were given her; but it did not prevent her from asking continually new questions respecting the generous stranger, who had unquestionably been the first instrument in effecting her deliverance.

As the count seemed averse to giving her the desired information, she ceased to urge him, and endeavoured to conceal her dissatisfaction, that she might not appear to repay with ingratitude the affection shown her by her new father. Münster, who, at the request of Ida, had been permitted to remain in the apartment, was silent and reserved, fearful of exciting the jealousy of the count; and the count found the caresses of his daughter cold in comparison with what he expected. Thus they parted for the night, pleased with having escaped past dangers, and looking forward to new enjoyments; though the sensations they felt were not altogether unmixed with bitterness.

CHAPTER II.

IDA received orders no more to quit the house of her father, and was conducted to her chamber, happy at length to be able to repose herself, and collect her scattered ideas, after a day of such extraordinary adventures. She soon dismissed her attendants, and flung herself dressed as she was, into a chair, to reflect anew on the incidents that had happened to her in so short a space of time. A gentle noise at the door interrupted her meditations, and instantly a man made his appearance. At first she was alarmed, and would have fled and called her servants : but the person who entered fell at her feet, laid hold of her gown, and with a voice that penetrated her inmost soul, supplicated her for a moment to listen to him.—" What voice do I hear?" exclaimed Ida: " whom do I see! . . . . " Herman ! " O Heavens! . . . ."

" Yes, princess, it is Herman. You
" see him compelled to be rash, to be im-
" portunate. But he must speak to you
" now, or forego the hope of it for ever."
Saying this, he gently shut the door, and
approached Ida, who stood resting with her
hand on a table, experiencing at once the
opposite sentiments of uneasines and joy,
and not knowing how to act.

A young woman familiarised with the
customary ceremonials of virtue, would
have been offended at the step taken by Herman, or at least would have appeared so to
be. To be alone with a lover at midnight,
and the door shut, was surely enough to
taint with suspicion the most unblemished
reputation : but Ida, in the first transports
of her joy, thought not of consequences
like these. Bending towards Herman, who
had embraced her knees, she held out her
arms, then suddenly drew them back, confused and blushing. The young knight too
well guessed her intention, not to avail himself of it. He took courage therefore, and

folded her in his arms; but, dissatisfied with her conduct, she soon disengaged herself, and ran to a door, which led, she supposed, to the apartment of her women. Herman followed her, and they found themselves in a balcony, beyond which they could not pass.

"Ah! do not fly from me!" said he : "do not reduce me to despair!. I must "speak to you, and I hope you have suf- "ficient confidence in me to believe, that I "would not have sought you at such an "hour, had I any other means of inform- "ing you of what it is absolutely necessary "you should know, before a long and per- "haps eternal separation."

"An eternal separation!" said Ida, interrupting him, and casting her eyes on the ground.

"Yes, an eternal separation from him, "whom once you looked on with an eye of "favor. And has your exaltation so speedily "changed your sentiments?"

"Herman." exclaimed Ida, in the most impassioned tone, "you know me not.

" Changed! changed with every respect to
" him, who, when I was so much his in-
" ferior, loved me so . . . .

" Say so ardently, so tenderly," continued the youth, finding her hesitate; " and
" who, were you sovereign of the world,
" could not love you otherwise than he
" loved you when Ida Munster: when . . ."

" Stop:" said the princess, with a look
of severity. " Regard to my honor re-
" quires, that your visit should be as short
" as possible: leave this subject, therefore,
" and hasten to tell me that which you say
" it is so necessary I should know."

Herman obeyed. They seated themselves in the balcony, which commanded a
fine prospect over a retired garden, then en-
lightened by the moon, and he thus began:

" It is incumbent upon me to warn you
" not to confide too securely in your pre-
" sent happiness. You saw what happened
" to me when I undertook your defence
" before the secret tribunal . . . . ."

" What !" exclaimed Ida, " was it you,
" that would have died for me? You, that
" risked every thing to save me, when aban-
" doned by all the world besides? O Hea-
" vens! shall I ever be capable . . . ..? No
" never!" A flood of tears then fell from
her eyes: she raised her hands to Heaven,
and cast on Herman a look, that forcibly
expressed the emotions of her heart.

" You did not know it then? You were
" not informed of it? —— In this I clearly
" perceive the character of the count: and
" you see what we have . . . pardon me, I
" meant to say . . . . what I have to expect
" from him."   ·

" You must tell me, Herman, every
" thing that has passed, from the moment
" of our separation.   The night is long;
" we are alone; nobody will interrupt us."

Ida seemed totally to have forgotten
what she had said a minute before, that regard to her honour required his visit to be
brief, and Herman had no great desire of
reminding her of it.

" When I took leave of you, at Mun-
" ster's," resumed our hero, " or rather,
" when you had quitted me, cruel as ap-
" peared to me the necessity of separating
" myself from every thing I held dear in the
" world, there yet remained for me another
" severe stroke, to be inflicted by her, whom
" whom you called your mother. It was
" she who gave me the first intimation of
" what you have lately learnt, and of which
" no one is now ignorant; that it was not
" without reason you possessed that dignity
" of mien, that announces exalted rank;
" and that you really were, what you ap-
" peared to be, the daughter of a prince.
" The haste in which she was obliged to
" impart to me this secret, and the presence
" of Munster, who narrowly watched us,
" prevented my hearing the name of the
" happy mortal, who had a right to call you
" his daughter; and thus I found myself
" more uncertain than ever of what I had to
" hope.. But we are ever ready to flatter
" ourselves; and I confess, however by

" birth you might be exalted above me,
" that I was not deterred from relying on
" my courage and on my sword, which I
" trusted would one day enable me to look
" up to the daughter of a prince with confi-
" dence. Vast projects then opened to my
" mind: I lost myself in reverie, and forgot
" every thing; so that I was at some distance
" from Prague when I recollected the request
" of your supposed mother, the good Mrs.
" Munster, who, when she bid me adieu,
" had urged me to remain another day,
" in order to second a step she meant to
" undertake in your favour with the empe-
" ror. I returned to Prague; thence re-
" paired to Conradsbourg; and thence to
" numerous other places, to which I was
" sent by persons who were playing the fool
" with me. I could meet with the empe-
' ror no where. My unexpected return;
" after having formally taken leave, and the
" anxiety I displayed, excited curiosity, and
" exposed me to malicious remarks. The
" not being able to acquit myself better,

" and with less delay, of an affair that relat-
" ed to you, urged me to desperation. It
" might have concerned your birth, which
" possibly Mrs. Munster wished to reveal;
" it might have required the utmost promp-
" titude; I was altogether in ignorance of
" what was to be done ; and my extraordina-
" ry behaviour occasioned probably the
" strange report which was circulated or my
" being bereft of my senses: a report
" which I first heard from the secret tribunal
" when it was alledged as one of the accusa-
" tions against you.

" I imagined I had still one friend, at
" court, and of him I at length obtained an
" audience. He advised me to depart from
" the country with speed, as my life was not
" in fafety, and assured me, that he would
" discharge my commission as faithfully as I
" could do it myself. I have since learnt,
" that this was intended to frighten me, in
" order to keep me from the court, as the
" emperor, from whom at first my return
" had been concealed, having at length

" heard of it, expressed a wish to speak
" with me.   I had long been envied the
" feeble remains of the favour I once enjoy-
" ed with him; and the eager pursuers of
" his smiles feared, that I should regain my
" former influence, if I made my appearance
" anew.   They sought, therefore, to drive
" me away, by the pretence, that there was a
" design against my life; and, to put an
" end to the questions of Winceslaus, con-
" cerning me, they spread a report of my
" my death, which you know passed for
" certain even with the judges of the secret
" tribunal, who pretend to be ignorant of
" nothing.

" I was thus induced to resume my jour-
" ney towards the court of king Sigismond.
" There I found my old friend, Nicholas
" Gara, the Hungarian general, under whom
" I had served against the rebels of Prague,
" but the extent of whose power I now first
" learned.   With joy he received me into
" his suit.   The court of Hungary was pre-
" paring for a war against the Turks.   Si-

" gismond had lost his consort, the good
" queen Mary, who was exceedingly beloved
" and with her more than half the affections
" of his people. He was suspected even,
" by his ill treatment, or at least by his want
" of kindness, of having occasioned her
" death. He was hated: the debaucheries
" of his court were made the subjects of pas-
" quinades; they styled him a second Win-
" ceslaus; and though, as I then believed,
" he deserved but in part these reproaches,
" he found himself under the necessity of
" endeavouring to obliterate such unpleasing
" impressions by some splendid atchieve-
" ments, that would add lustre to his repu-
" tation. A war against the infidels he
" considered as the surest way of attaining
" his purpose, and in consequence he resolv-
" to unite with those who had sworn them-
" selves enemies to the standard of
" Mohammed.

" What a prospect for one whose aim
" was bent on glory, in order to merit Ida!
" What laurels did I not hope to gather,

" to what heights did I not aspire, that I
" might raise myself, celestial maid, to an
" equality with thee! No prince I thought
" would hesitate to choose me for his son-
" in-law, when, covered with the blood of
" the infidels, and enriched with their spoils.
" I returned to the court of Sigismond, to
" fill the brilliant offices, with which my
" vanity, relying on the attachment of my
" friend Gara, flattered my imagination.—
" And perhaps these hopes would have been
" realised, had I been willing blindly to
" close with the projects of this general, who
" had every thing in his disposal.

" Our march was begun, and we joined
" the enemies of the grand Signior. We
" We attacked him vigorously, performed
" prodigies of valour, yet seldom came off
" conquerors. Some malignant deity seem-
" ed to reign over our fate, and to snatch
" victory from our hands, even at the mo-
" ment we thought it secure.

" Our ill success was ascribed to the se-
" cret crimes of the king; and the general

" seemed to countenance such seditious dis-
" course. I had good reason before to
" suspect, that Gara endeavoured to defeat
" the designs of his master by secretly fa-
" vouring the enemy. My suspicion was
" converted into certainty, when he dis-
" closed to me the hatred he bore the king,
" and attempted to detach me from his in-
" terest. He was the eldest son of old Ni-
" cholas Gara, whom Sigismond had for-
" merly beheaded. He therefore breathed
" nothing but vengeance against the mur-
" derer of his father; nor could Sigismond
" have been guilty of a greater imprudence,
" than to commit to one of the sons of the
" deceased, the supreme power over the
" army, and to the other, Andrew Gara,
" the regency of the realm during his ab-
" sence. But the principal features in Si-
" gismond's character are openness, magna-
" nimity, and imprudence. He delights
" to make reparation for his faults, and he
" loaded his enemies with honours, think-
" ing thereby to render them his friends.

VOL. II. C

" The ill intentions of the general became
" to me daily more evident. I loved the
" king with all my soul; and I shewed
" Gara, without disguise, the horror I felt
" at his proposal to assist him in dethroning
" his master. Had not my youth and in-
" experience blinded me, I had, at the
" commencement of our acquaintance, suf-
" ficient reasons to suspect his integrity.
" Was it not he, who had formerly dared
" to justify Winceslaus for his execrable
" murder of the principal inhabitants of
" Prague!

" I concealed not from Gara the opi-
" nion I conceived of him. My sincerity
" displeased him; he grew cool towards me;
" imputed to me imaginary faults; ceased
" to promote me; went even so far as to
" take from me the offices I held, to bestow
" on me others inferior to them; and at
" length I received permission to quit the
" army. As it was however but a permis-
" sion, not an order, I paid no regard to it,
" choosing rather to serve my king in the

" capacity of a common soldier, than co-
" wardly to leave him in the hands of his
" enemies. Heavens! how much did I
" wish to inform him of the perfidy that
" was hatching against him! But how was it
" to be done? All his steps, as well as mine,
" were watched; he had also been preju-
" diced against me; and it was impossible
" for me to speak to him in private.

" Meanwhile I shall ever retain the
" pleasing remembrance of having had it
" in my power to render him a signal ser-
" vice, before my destiny separated me
" from him. According to custom, we had
" fought bravely against the infidels, without
" obtaining the victory. To lose the battle
" was unavoidable, for so it pleased Nicholas
" Gara. The duke of Burgundy had al-
" ready fallen into the hands of the Turks,
" and a similar fate threatened the king.
" His attendants had deserted him, and
" left him engaged in single combat with
" the valiant Achmet, who was far his su-
" perior. I had received orders from the

C 2

" general to retire, and repair to another
" post.   But I was deaf to his command,
" collected twenty loyal Hungarians, and
" extricated Sigismond from his perilous
" situation.

" " How did I regret, that I was obliged
" almost the same instant to quit him! But
" love called me, and I was unable to resist
" the summons.   The danger you ran,
" dear Ida, had reached my ears : I felt the
" the necessity of saving you, and the at-
" tachment I bore my king yielded to the
" more powerful sentiment with which you
" had inspired me. I left Sigismond, how-
" ever, in the protection of such faithful
" subjects that no one durst openly attempt
" any thing against his person. . I would
" have taken this opportunity of informing
" him of the snares that were spread for
" him, had he been capable of listening to
" me ; but he was grievously wounded, and
" had a considerable fever, which affected
" his brain.   In consequence I charged his
" loyal attendants to communicate to him

" what I could not, and with speed I repair-
" ed to you : . . . to you, whom I knew to
" be threatened by the pitiless arm of the
" secret tribunal."

" May I ask," said the princess, interrupting him, " how, at so great a diſtance,
" you heard of my misfortune ?"

" It is a circumstance I do not yet fully
" understand myself : however, I will ex-
" plain it to you as well as I can.   You
" doubtless remember old Andrew, whom
" Munster gave me for my esquire, on my
" departure from Prague ?"

" Certainly I do.   There were more
" persons than one in our house who re-
" joiced at the circumstance, as it freed
" them from the inspection of a vigilant spy,
" whom nothing escaped.   Me you as-
" suredly will not rank in the number of
" the persons who hated him : on the con-
" trary, I esteemed him for his fidelity ;
" though, I confess, his simplicity was so
" singularly contrasted with traits of appa-
" rent art and cunning, which sometimes

C 3

" escaped him from want of attention, that
" I was at a loss what to think of him."

" I made myself precisely the same re-
" mark, on his conduct, and he gave me a
" thousand occasions for repeating them.
" You shall hear by what extraordinary
" means he became the primary cause of
" my sudden appearance before you, and,
" if I may be permitted so to say, of your
" deliverance."

" We were arming for battle, the day
" on which, as I have just mentioned to
" you, I had the happiness to save the life
" of the king.   Andrew, who commonly,
" in spite of his age, yielded not in courage
" and intrepidity to the most resolute of
" our youth, appeared, while buckling on
" my armour, sad and dejected. ' Sir,'
" said he, ' the road we are about to take
" may lead to the tomb. It is possible I
" may fall, and where can I die better than
" in the field of honour? But in case it
" should happen, I ought to inform you of
" something which it imports you to know.

" When the battle is over, do not stay long
" in this country; I have a presentiment,
" that things do not go so well as they ought
" in the house of, my old master. The
" life of a person who is not indifferent to
" you is in danger.' I looked at him
" steadily, and asked the reason of his ap-
" prehensions: but he refused to explain
" himself more clearly, resumed his wonted
" air of simplicity, and attributed what he
" had said to some melancholy dream.

" Though I was never weak enough to
" have faith in such things, I yet was a little
" disturbed at what he said, and I put to
" him fresh quetions. ' Let us drop the
" subject for the present,' replied Andrew:
" ' we have now to meet the enemy: If I
" never return, you know enough: if I do,
" you will know more.'

" The attack commenced. Andrew
" was one of the first who fell by my side.
" I directed him to be carried out of the
" throng, that his wounds might be dressed.
" The principal events of the battle I have

C 4

" related; but I have not told you, that the
" first news I heard, after quitting the tent
" of Sigismond, was the death of poor An-
" drew. His comrade, who came to ac-
" quaint me with it, told me, that as he
" was dying, he spoke of a certain lady of
" the name of Ida, and charged him to tell
" me to hasten to her succour, as she was
" in danger of perishing by the secret tri-
" bunal. At the same time he delivered
" me a billet, which the dying man had
" taken from his bosom, and directed him
" to give me, as it would inform me of the
" time I had for my journey, and the place
" where you would be found. You may
" easily conceive the eagerness with which
" I set off, without staying for further in-
" telligence.

" I did not reflect on the circumstances
" of this strange adventure till afterwards;
" when I was led to believe Andrew to have
" belonged to that formidable society, the
" members of which, spread over the earth,
" are informed, almost in the twinkling of

" an eye, of what passes in the most distant
" parts of their invisible empire, as if they
" were connected together by some magic
" chain. You have seen how numerous are
" the judges and associates of this tribunal;
" and I have reason to believe, that it has
" more adherents among the people, than
" among the nobility. " Those of the
" former class constitute the links of that
" immense chain, the secret wheels of that
" fearful engine, with the thousand eyes of
" which the SEERS, as they call themselves,
" obtain knowledge of every thing that is
" done, and discover mysteries that seem
" impenetrable. I doubt not but Andrew
" was one of the associates of this class;
" but attachment to the family of his an-
" cient master led him, as far as he could,
" to overstep the limits of that religious
" silence to which he was bound by his
" oath.

" I travelled on, without well knowing
" in what consisted the danger that threaten-
" ed you, and consequently what was to be.

C 5

" done to extricate you from it. During
" my journey, nothing was talked of but
" your adventure. In every town and vil-
" lage I saw stuck up against the buildings
" an invitation to undertake your defence;
" and I soon learnt the conduct I had to
" pursue. There were two days still to in-
" tervene between the time of my arrival
" and that of your trial. These I spent in
" the manner pointed out to me by a man
" of the name of Walter, with whom chance
" brought me acquainted. I would have
" waited on you at your convent, but he
" dissuaded me, saying, that no one was ad-
" mitted to defend a person accused before
" the secret tribunal, unless he could prove,
" that there had not been the most distant
" connection between him and the party
" for the space of a year. By Walter I was
" further informed, that you had nobody
" to accompany you to the appointed place
" whither the stranger came to fetch you;
" and, as it was forbidden me to offer you
" my hand, I planted myself on the road

" you were to take, that I might. secretly
" watch over and protect you from insult.
" I saw you pass, accompanied by the nuns,
" and if any thing could have augmented
" the opinion I had formed of you, it must
" have been the venerable attendance of
" those pious maidens, who, by the attention
" they paid you, showed in a striking man-
" ner their persuasion of your innocence;
" and I have also since learnt, that this pro-
" cedure of the nuns made no small im-
" pression on your judges."

  " And yet," said Ida, interrupting him,
" my eloquent defender was refused a hear-
" ing. Matters were carried so far, that he
" was arrested as a criminal, which, I sup-
" posed, would render my justification im-
" possible. I could not support the cruel
" idea; I swooned at that dreadful moment;
" and even now .... when I think of
" it ...."

  " Who can explain all the manœuvres
" of people who are themselves a mistery?"
said Herman to the pensive and dejected

Ida. " For my part, I cannot; and, even
" if I could, I still should not dare. Whilst
" you were insensible, you were carried
" away, and the person who brought you to
" the tribunal set you down at the place
" where he had received you from the hands
" of the nuns: I know, however, that he
" secretly watched over your safety. In
" the mean time I was interrogated, and
" treated with rigour. I had said, that you
" were the daughter of a prince, and I was
" required to prove it. Of the faet I had
" no farther certainty than the assertion of
" Mrs. Munster. The chief of the tribu-
" nal then rose, drew near to me, and, in
" a tone of voice that betrayed the greatest
" emotion, put to me questions, which I
" knew not how to answer. I had been
" stripped, as is customary on such occa-
" sions, and conducted before the judges
" with my head and feet bare, and my bo-
" dy wrapped round with woollen cloth.
" My cloaths had been examined, and the
" chain you formerly gave me was in the

" hands of the president. . This chain was.
" one principal subject of his questions.
" He asked, 'How I came by it: if I knew
" count Everard of Wirtemberg, whose
" portrait was fastened to it: if I had not
" received with it a ring also: if I knew
" the party accused: if I had ever observed
" on her left hand a small mark, resem-
" bling a cross: and if I could not guess
" the name of the prince whose daughter
" she was?' All these questions I answered
" briefly and ingenuously; as well as many
" others, particularly the following: 'Why
" I defended you with so much warmth:
" whether I loved you: whether I had any
" hopes: whether I had spoken to you
" lately, &c.' At length I was set at liberty,
" and my cloaths were returned; but they
" kept the precious jewel which I received
" from your hand, and which, according
" to appearance, was the token by which
" you were known.

" I was ordered not to quit the city,
" and to appear again the moment I should

" be cited. This however, has not taken
" place; and I have just learnt, in a way
" which I am not at liberty to disclose,
" that last night the secret tribunal met
" once more on your affair, when the chief
" arose from his throne, and answered for
" your innocence, on his terrible oath, af-
" ter which you were formally acquitted
" of every accusation.

    " On the other hand, I was this morn-
" ing sent for by the count of Wirtemberg,
" who gave me a very flattering reception,
" informed me, that the young person I had
" so ably defended, was discovered to be
" his daughter, and, in recompence of the
" service I had rendered him, offered me
" a present that did honor to his generosity.
" But, alas! the words that accompanied it,
" were far from being equally generous.

    " 'I am not surprised,' said he, ' at
" your having loved the charming Ida Mun-
" ster: it was natural, and suitable to your
" station. I hope, however, that you will
" henceforth cease to think of a person,

"whom fortune has raised so eminently
" above you, and with whom it is impossi-
" ble you should have the slightest inter-
" course? particulary as you are of the fa-
" mily of Unna, and consequently related
" to him who attacked count Everard at
" Wisbaden.'—The answer I made your
" proud father, was dictated by the rage
" that possessed me. We parted highly
" displeased with each other. He sent me
" his humiliating present, which I instantly
" returned. In no case would I have ac-
" cepted a reward for saving your life, and
" much less in this."

Herman had risen from his seat, and
was walking with hasty strides backwards
and forwards in the balcony. Ida perceived how much he was offended; she was herself also extremely agitated, if not by anger,
at least by secret dissatisfaction, which prevented her speaking, lest she should betray
the sentiments she felt.

" Sir," said she at length, with a trembling voice, " I imagine you have finished

" the recital of your adventures : day is on
" the point of appearing; we must part;
" and you have not yet informed me of the
" motive of your visit.   You said, that you
" had to tell me of a danger with which I
" was threatened, or . . . ."

" Oh Ida !" cried Herman, approaching
her, with an accent of the most endearing
tenderness : " Do you perceive no danger
" in what I have related ? If there be none
" to you, to me at least there is that of an
" eternal separation.   And is the fate of
" him to whom you . . . . is the fate of
" Herman become so indifferent to you ?
" Meanwhile," continued he, whilst Ida
timidly drew back from him, " this is not
" all I have to tell you : hear what has hap-
" pened to me to-day, and judge what you
" have to do.

" When I quitted the count, your fa-
" ther, though he deserved not the appel-
" lation, I met the honest Munster.   Alas!
" he too has treated me with severity, yet
" I would to heaven you were still his

" daughter! I related to him what had pas-
" sed between me and him, of whom my
" lips wish not to pronounce the 'name; and
" I was desirous also of giving him an ac-
" count of what had previously happened
" to me, but he appeared to be in a great
" measure already acquainted with it. At
" length he took me home with him, and
" satisfied all my questions concerning you,
" as far as was in his power. His sole mo-
" tive for quitting you so hastily at the con-
" vent, was to go in quest of me, to demand
" the chain, which you informed him was
" in my possession, and which was necessa-
" ry to prove your birth. But soon relin-
" quishing this design, the execution of
" which would have required too much time
" he formed another project for your deli-
" verance. I cannot say, 'with certainty,
" what this project was, as he did not fully
" explain himself on the subject. As far
" however as I can judge from appearances,
" it is probable he took some steps to be
" admitted into the number of associates of

" the secret tribunal, as he had heard, that
" an oath taken by a free judge, in affirma-
" tion of the innocence of a person accused,
". was sufficient for his acquittal. Munster
". was little aware of the difficulty of being
". admitted a member of this terrible tribu-
". nal; that it was previously necessary to be
" put to the proof, and to fill inferior sta-
" tions, before he could arrive to any influ-
" ence in it: and this required time, where-
" as your situation demanded the most spee-
" dy succour. But as he had taken the
" first steps, he could not be permitted to
" retract, and was kept in confinement.—
" Unable, therefore, to seek any means of
" delivering his dear Ida, he found himself
" obliged to abandon to Providence her
" fate.

    " At this juncture I arrived. He knew
" that I was here, yet was not at liberty to
" speak to me. I declared to the judges,
" what I had heard of your birth. He, who
" had hitherto passed for your father, was
" interrogated on the subject, and obliged to

" appear before the count of Wirtemberg,
" who, in all appearance, is the chief of
" the secret tribunal in this district; for I
" I perfectly recollect his voice and gait, in
" spite of his disguise.

" The answers of Munster removed
" every doubt respecting your birth; and
" the count was so firmly convinced of the
" innocence of his daughter, that he hesi-
" tated not an instant to make himself re-
-" sponsible for it. What has since been
" executed, was then resolved on, and you
" were set free. The greater part of this
" account I have received from a person
" whom I dare not name, for the discourses
" of the reserved Munster turned chiefly on
" the necessity of renouncing you, and the
" impossibility of my attachment ever be-
" ing crowned with success.

" ' You know,' said he, ' the observa-
" tions I often made on the subject, when
" you believed me to be the father of Ida :
" you would not then give credit to them,
" yet now you must be convinced they were

" well-founded. I will not enquire whe-
" ther a princess of Wirtemberg be too ele-
" vated a match for you: but you cannot
" conceal from yourself the determined en-
" mity of count Everard to your house.
" Though you took no part in the affair of
" Wi-baden, he will never forgive you, for
" the crimes of your relations. Beside, he
" has other views for his daughter. As he
" has little hope himself of attaining the
" first dignity in the empire, he wishes at
" least to be allied to him, to whom it is
" probably destined. Now it is generally
" supposed, that duke Frederick of Bruns-
" wick, will one day afcend the throne of
" Bohemia ; and him therefore has count
" Everard chosen for his son-in-law.—
" Death lately deprived the count of a
" daughter, whose hand had been promised
" to the duke; it will therefore, he thinks,
" be easy to substitute Ida in her place;
" and as Ida is far superior in beauty, the
" execution of this scheme appears to him
" certain. After this, ' Would you prevent

" the happiness of her you love? Would
" you take from her the prospect of wear-
" ing the first diadem in the world?'

" I will not repeat to you, the answer I
" made: it is of little importance. But
" permit me, madam, to ask you one
" question: Are you inclined to give your
" hand to a prince, who knows you not?
" To a man, who, should he prefer you,
" will be determined only by reasons of
" state? To a man who having placed else-
" where his affections, despised and treated
" with neglect your sister, whose hand was
" offered to him, and probably caused her
" to die of grief? To a man, in short, who,
" if dazzled by your charms, though he
" may experience for you sentiments more
" tender than those with which she in-
" spired him, will not fail to give you
" rivals, who . . . ."

Redoubled knocks at the door of Ida's
chamber interrupted the conversation of
the two lovers, and alarmed them extremely. The princess hastily rushed from

the balcony, and ran to the door. Heavens! it was her father.

"What!" said he, with a look of asto- nishment: " so early! day scarcely broken, " and dressed already!"

" My father, I am .... I am accus- " tomed to rise early."

" You were in the balcony. Where are " your women? You were talking: are " you also accustomed to talk to yourself?"

These questions threw Ida into the most cruel perplexity; she knew not what she ought to say; and had her father put to her a single question more, he would have learnt all, that, under the present circumstances, it was so important to conceal from him. But fortunately, too eager to continue coolly this examination, he flew to the balcony. Finding no one there, he returned perfectly calm, and begged the trembling Ida, who durst not yet look up to him, no more to expose herself to the chill morning air, and still less to the tongue of calumny, by talk- ing to herself, as she had done. " The

" little sleep you have taken," added he,
" has made you pale; you have deranged
" my projects; I intended to-day to have
" presented you at court, but I perceive
" that you must have another day to re-
" cover yourself."

He then embraced her tenderly, and
begged her to go to bed again, as the sun
was scarcely risen, and she had need of
repose.

CHAPTER III.

SATISFIED at being so happily extricated from the aukward situation in which
she found herself, Ida ran to the balcony,
to see what was become of Herman. He
had disappeared. She could form no
conjecture, but he had ventured to leap
from it into the garden to escape the
count, whose voice he no doubt heard.
She looked down: all was quiet and motion-
less, except that, at a distance, she perceived
a centinel parading backwards and forwards,
which rendered her uneasy about the escape
of her lover, and the injury her reputation
might suffer. "Alas!" said she, with a
sigh, " must the great every where have
" witnesses of their moft secret actions?
" And can they never be permitted to do
" any thing without being observed, or at
" least without being under constraint?
" How preferable was the peaceful life I
" led in the house of Munster, to the hu-

" miliating confinement in which it appears
" I am to be held here; a confinement
" even greater than what I experienced at
" the court of the empress!"

Ida willingly followed the advice of her
father, in retiring to bed; for she had need
of repose: but the reflections that occupied
her mind, totally prevented her from sleeping. Having remained some time in bed
to no purpose, she at length resolved to rise
and call her women. That day she received no visit: the count of Wirtemberg
himself came to see her but for a moment.
She was melancholy and dejected, and durst
not compare her present situation with that
she had quitted, lest she should find the
comparison too unfavourable to the former.
The sole circumstances from which she derived consolation, were the thought of the
danger she had just escaped, and her present security; the shame and disgrace to
which she had been exposed, and her innocence now acknowledged: her heart then
palpitated with joy and gratitude to heaven,

VOL. II. D

and the person, whom next to heaven she considered as her saviour. The narrative of Herman afforded her matter for fresh reflections; and these were insensibly replaced by the tender remembrance of the empress, to whom she was next day to be presented. To behold Sophia, to see her again after being completely justified, to relate what she had suffered for love of her, and to humble her enemies by the lustre of her innocence and her rank, formed such a prospect, that Ida must have been more than woman, nay, more than mortal, to have been indifferent to its enjoyment.

The wished-for day appeared. Ida was dressed in a manner suitable to her rank. She was naturally beautiful; and the impression of her late sorrow, which was yet not entirely obliterated, served but to render her more interesting.

Count Everard had acquainted the empress with his intention of presenting to her his daughter. The princess of Ratibor was accordingly deputed to fetch the young

princess of Wirtemberg, in Sophia's state
coach, and to assure her of the impatience
with which she expected her. Who has
not seen, who does not know, how brazen
is the forehead of an experiencied courtier?
The princess of Ratibor felt no embarrassment from the commission with which she
was charged to her, whom she had so cruel-
ly-injured: and the sole vengeance that the
noble-minded Ida took of the impudence,
with which she pretended to participate in
her unexpected happiness, was a look of dis-
dainful pity, which she cast on her enemy.

The count, however, was not equally
forbearing. The character of envoy from
the empress, in which the princess of Ratibor appeared, had some restraint upon him;
but he said enough to remind her of the infamous part she had acted with regard to his
daughter; and the princess of Ratibor, for
the first time in her life, habituated as
she was to dissimulation, knew not how
to act.

D 2

The princess of Wirtemberg was received in the empress's anti-chamber by the duke of Bavaria. He embraced her, and made an apology for having been so slow in perceiving her innocence. The great have the privilege, or at least fancy they have the privilege, of making reparation for every injury by a few civil expressions. But Ida paid little attention to what was said by the duke, for her heart was on the wing to meet Sophia, who, still somewhat feeble from her illness, was sitting at the farther end of the chamber and, attempting to rise, held out her arms to her young friend.

The daughter of the count threw herself at her feet.—" Pure, spotless soul!" cried the empress, pressing her to her bosom: " how much hast thou suffered for the love " of me! how hast thou supported it? woe " to those who availed themselves of my " weak state, to seek the ruin of my best and " dearest frie..d."

Ida bathed the knees of her sovereign with her tears. " Rise," said Sophia, rise:

" that posture becomes only your persecu-
" tors. How I regret, that they are in reali-
" ty forced to pay to your rank that respect
" which they owe to your innocence; how
" I regret, that you are no longer Ida Mun-
" ster, that I might raise you to the height
" of my wishes! Why has fortune done
" what I could so ardently have desired to
" do for you myself!"

Joy rendered Sophia eloqent, while it
bereft Ida of words; probably because she
felt it more forcibly than the empress. In
fact, few persons were capable of loving like
her; and the lively remembrance of her
misfortunes, and her glorious deliverance
contributed, perhaps, still farther to height-
en the intensity of her feelings.

The empress ordered all the ladies of the
court to embrace the princess of Wirtemberg. The princess of Ratibor and her
daughter, whose yellow and livid visages betrayed the envy that inwardly gnawed their
hearts, presented themselves foremost; the
rest followed with an air of somewhat less

D 3

constraint; nor was there one, who did not assure the charming Ida, that she had obtained nothing more than she merited, and that, the day they first beheld her, they could not help confessing, that she was worthy of, and would do honor to the most elevated rank.

Sophia, who was not ignorant of their jealousies and secret persecutions, smiled with an air of disdain, and bade them retire, as she wished to be alone with the duke of Bavaria, count Everard and his daughter.

Our manuscript does not inform us, what subject engaged the attention of these four personages; but it says that the conversation did not become truly interesting till Sophia and Ida were left by themselves; and that then took place between them, all the reciprocal endearments, all the tender effusions, usually felt by two hearts, formed for each other, when, having been separated by misfortune, they find themselves happily reunited. Ida remarked too, though Sophia would not acquiesce in the truth of the observation, that her friend opened her heart with much less reserve to the princess of Wirtemberg, than to the humble Ida Munster, a discovery which it is not possible for us to say whether it afforded her greater pain or pleasure.

Certain however it is that this renewal of friendship so transported the new princess, that she hesitated not, in her turn, to disclose her inmost thoughts to Sophia; nor was even her love for Herman, or the late nocturnal visit he had paid her omitted: she allowed herself only a few alterations and curtailments, as there were circumstances in the case that related not to herself alone, and which she knew not how they might be received.

Sophia promised to favour with all her influence, her friend's attachment to Herman. Obliged to become the wife of Winceslaus, she had perhaps frequently lamented that she had not herself enjoyed the liberty of chusing a husband; it may be presumed, therefore, that she meant to keep her word, and that she was anxious to

D 4

devise the surest means of arriving at the desired end.

Ida's ascendency over the empress was unbounded, and she could do with her as she pleased. By her recommendation Munster was called to court and loaded with favours: a circumstance by no means to be wondered at, when we consider the grateful and feeling heart of her who had so long thought herself his daughter, and which we should scarcely have mentioned, had it not led to a recital which we shall no longer detain from the reader. Sophia was as curious as perhaps, he may be, to hear the history of the infancy of her friend, and the manner in which she had been taken from her parents; and one day, therefore, when Munster found himself alone with Ida and the empress, they requested him to relate the particulars of this history, a request with with which he complied, as will be seen in the following chapter.

CHAPTER IV.

History of the Infancy of Ida.

" O PRINCESS," said Munster, after some moments of reflection, " what a task " do you impose upon a man who values so " highly your affection, and the favour of " the empress! You require me to confess " faults that will perhaps ruin me in your " esteem. They have plunged you into " an abyss of misfortune, and have no " other excuse but my blind regard for a " woman, who, beautiful as Eve, might " well seduce to evil a frail child of Adam. " You, Ida, know her whom you believed " to be your mother, and can judge, from " what she is now, how beautiful she must " have been at four and twenty. I loved " her; but the difference of our conditions " rendered my happiness next to impossi- " ble. I was one of the principle officers " of the count of Wirtemberg, and Maria

D 5

" was a vassal. Become at so early an age
" a widow, the death of her husband and
" of her only child, an infant at the breast,
" excited compassion, and she was taken
" into the service of the countess, as the
" nurse of her daughter. Ida was but a
" few weeks old when her mother died.—
" Maria, before the death of her mistress,
" had been promised her liberty, and the
" office of nurse to the young princess giv-
" ing her a farther claim to the favour, in-
" creased the hopes of my love.

   " Unfortunately the welfare of their
" dependants is generally deemed of too
" trivial importance to merit the attention
" of princes. A single word would have
" made two human beings happy, and fix-
" ed indelible impressions of gratitude in
" our hearts: but that word was withheld.
" I was sent to a distance from the place
" where the object of my wishes resided;
" and she was treated with a severity that
" excited in her breast feelings of hatred,
" and urged her to a step, which, had she

" not been provoked by ill treatment, she
" would never have taken.

" The charming little Ida, admired by
" every body, and adored by her nurse,
" was scarcely two years old, when the de-
" ceased countess of Wittemberg was alrea-
" dy forgotten, and the count had chosen,
" to fill her place, a young woman whose
" beauty and rank were her only preten-
" sions.

" Her sentiments were sufficiently un-
" generous to separate from the title of wife
" of count Everard, that of mother to his
" children. She loved, or at least pretend-
" ed to love, the first, while the others she
" detested. Maria, who contrived some-
" times the means of writing to me by
" stealth, acquainted me with the evil pro-
" ceedings of this step-mother. The sons
" of her husband, who began to grow up,
" were sent to the army, equipped in a
" manner unsuitable to their rank. No
" attention was paid to their youth and in-
" experience which demanded some indul-

"gence. His daughters were shamefully
" obtruded upon inferior princes, who mar-
" ried them solely from the consideration of
" their birth. It was evidently the inten-
" tion of the new countess to encrease her
" fortune at the expence of the children of
" her husband. The youngest but one of
" these children, died for want of care, and
" Maria did not fail to impute to the wick-
" edness of the step-mother this accident as
" well as the ill health of Ida, whom, she as-
" serted, it was the wish of the countess pri-
" vately to get rid of: accusations perhaps
" totally devoid of proof, and which nothing
" but the infatuation of love could have in-
" duced me to credit.

" One day I was invited by Maria, to
" repair secretly to the count's in order to
" advise with her about the means of saving
" her little favourite, and removing the ob-
" stacles that opposed themselves to our
" union. The latter became daily more
" difficult, from the severity of the countess,
" who continually protracted the emancipa-

" tion of Maria, and, at last, absolutely re-
" fused to consent to it.

" The letter which she sent me was
" dated at Wisbaden, where the count then
" resided with his court. He had retired
" thither, after the long, and in some respects,
" unfortunate war he had waged with the
" imperial cities, in order to enjoy a little
" repose. As I had positive orders from
" my master, not to quit the place where I
" was stationed, it was necessary that my
" arrival should be concealed; so that we
" could meet only at night, when we had no
" other witness than the little Ida, who,
" since the pregnancy of her step-mother,
" was less noticed than ever. She was kept
" shut up like a prisoner, with her nurse,
" in a remote apartment, where they were
" frequently suffered to be in want almost of
" the necessaries of life.

" Our secret conversations were not
" solely occupied by the unfortunate cir-
" cumstances of our attachment. The des-
" tiny of Ida was much more alarming to

"Maria than her own. 'Munster,' said
" she, ' you must not flatter yourself that I
" will ever assent to any project for our
" union, till this infant is in safety. You
" must either save us both, or renounce me
" for ever. 'Poor little innocent,' added
" she, pressing Ida to her bosom, who was
" asleep in her arms, 'shall I abandon
" thee! shall I leave thee in the hands of
" thy step-mother! shall I suffer the feeble
" spark of life that remains in thee to be
" extinguished by neglect. Look, my
" friend, at this pale and emaciated coun-
" tenance! Who would suppose it to be
" the little cherub, the once rosy and
" healthful Ida? And yet she eats nothing
" that I do not prepare with my own hands.
" No doubt the air we breathe in this place
" is empoisoned. I dread the very looks
" of this abominable countess, lest they
" should wither this delicate flower. It is
" true that, at present, she avoids the child;
" but should she seek her, I should shudder

" at her perfidious caresses, thinking every
" embrace was intended to stifle her.'

" Love and mistrust sharpened the feel-
" ings of Maria. Every day she fancied
" that she discovered new proofs of the
" countess's cruelty, and maintained, that
" when she became a mother, things would
" be worse; that the count would feel him-
" self less interested than at present for the
" fate of his daughter, and that she would
" indubitably be sacrificed to the offspring
" of her step-mother.

" It was easy to divine what were Maria's
" intentions. She wished that, by some
" daring attempt, I should procure her
" her liberty, and save the princess from the
" danger that impended over her, by taking
" her with us. On these conditions alone
" would she give me her hand. I loved the
" little Ida, but I could not resolve to steal
" her from her father, and thus deprive
" her of the rights of her birth. Things
" did not appear so desperate as Maria had
" represented. I attributed part of her ap-

" prehensions to her extreme fondness for
" the child, and her no less ardent anti-
" pathy to her who occupied the place of
" her former mistress, towards whom she
" preserved the firmest attachment.   I
" hoped that the fate of the young princess
" would be meliorated in a way more ho-
" nourable and just; and I resolved never
" to commit a theft, which I considered as
" of the number of those that ought never
" to be pardoned.

   " An unexpected event induced me to
" change my opinion, and realised the pro-
" ject of Maria, without its being necessary
" to take the smallest precaution. What
" shall I say? Love and compassion van-
" quished my scruples; I was imposed on
" by the semblance of an order from Hea-
" ven; my mistress was sufficiently adroit
" to avail herself of my weakness; and I
" determined on that dangerous step, which
" has since occasioned me such pangs of re-
" morse, and the princess such a multitude

" of evils; a step of which,. I trust, the
".melancholy consequences are now at
" an end.

" Afraid of oeing known, I had taken
" up my residence at the distance of a
" league from Wisbaden. Every evening,
" as soon as it was dark, I set out to visit
" Maria, and that I might not be surprised
" by the approach of day, returned after
" a conversation of a few hours, assuredly
" the happiest of my life. I constantly, in
" my way, passed through a forest, consi-
" dered by the country people as the haunt
" of malignant spirits, and which I should
" never have dared to enter, had I not
" been supported by the invincible courage
" that love can inspire. Indeed I had par-
" ticular,reasons to avoid it, as frequently
" things had happened to me there, for
" which I knew,not how to account.

" God knows, said I more than once to
" Maria, what passes in the bosom of that
" forest. Lonesome as it is by day, at
" night it swarms with living beings. I hear

" in it a confused hum of voices, spectres
" pass and repass: sometimes they come so
" near, that they seem to touch me. But,
" thank Heaven, they do no injury to the
" harmless traveller; so I let them pass,
" cross myself, and pretend not to see
" them.

"One night that I had quitted Maria
" earlier than usual, on account of the in-
" disposition of Ida, which would not per-
" mit us to have any conversation; I made
" a discovery, that removed my doubts re-
" specting that solitary wood.

" It was one of those dark nights in au-
" tumn, when the fogs are so thick as to-
" tally to obscure the light both of the
" moon and stars. A dank vapour over-
" spread the earth; I walked as in a cloud;
" and could perceive nothing but occasional
" sparks of fire, rising suddenly into the
" air, which might be occasioned, I thought,
" by an *ignis fatuus*, or something still worse.

" I was blindly groping out the path I
" had so frequently trod, when stumbling

" against a tree, I fell prostrate on the
" ground. I rose to resume my way, but
" soon found I had totally lost the track I had
" hitherto persued. Fearing that I should
" plunge deeper in the forest, and fall into
" some of the dangerous places with which
" I had been told it abounded, I resolved to
" wait for day, and pass the night on the
" spot where I was, endeavouring to collect
" for my couch what dry branches I could
" find in the dark.

" I had scarcely rested myself an hour,
" when I heard the noise, that had so fre-
" quently alarmed me, and which at a
" distance resembled the march of a body
" of men clad in armour. They seemed to
" approach, to separate, to rest, and then to
" begin their march again. I fancied they
" took different roads, and soon I distin-
" guished the voices of two of those beings,
" whom I had hitherto supposed to be
" sprites. They stopped just behind the
" bush, under which I was lying; and I
" then found, that those voices, of which

" the echo of the wood had conveyed to
" my ears but inarticulate sounds, pro-
" nounced a language like my own. This
" discovery changed my opinion, concern-
" ing the nature of the persons with whom
" I had to deal, for I had always conceived,
" that the peaceable inhabitants of the invi-
" sible world must have some other mode of
" communicating their ideas, than the use
" of human speech.

 " My courage now began to return; I
" listened with eager attention, that my ears
" might supply the deficiency of my eyes;
" and I was soon completely convinced,
" that those phantoms, at which I had been
" so often intimidated, were no other than
" men like myself. They complained of
" the badness of the weather, cursed their
" masters, and expressed their impatience
" for the arrival of day. I was on the point
" of discovering myself, that I might
" abridge the tediousness of the night by
" conversation, when a few words which
" they dropped made me first wish to know

" more concerning them, and in conse-
" quence I endeavoured to approach
" nearer.

" ' What noise did I hear?' cried one of
" them. ' Something certainly stirred be-
" hind the bush. Is the man, who crosses
" the wood, gone by?'

" ' Once,' answered the other : ' and
" he commonly does not return till near
" sun rise. Besides, he never does harm
" to any body, so you have nothing to fear,
" even were it he.'

" ' But perhaps, it is John Herdsman,
" who, they say, was executed here —
" Wherever I meet him, I turn out of his
" way, and pray for his soul.'

" ' May God forgive him!' resumed
" the second in a tone of affright : ' See!
" he is dressed in white, except that his col-
" lar is stained with blood. Poor soul!
" perhaps he was innocent.'

" These words, and some others similar
" to them, induced me to believe, that my
" neighbours were talking of me. My

" white cloak with a red collar was plainly
" described, and I could not avoid laughing
" to myself, to think I was acting the part
" of sprite to those, who had so long
" acted it toward me.

    " ' Did not I hear the spirit laugh?'
" continued one of them. ' He is endea-
" vouring to provoke us: let us get out of
" his way.'

    " ' We dare not quit our station; you
" know we must wait here for our masters.'

    " ' Are they gone again, do you think,
" to Wisbaden?'

    " ' Yes: God knows what will be the
" end of this enterprise.'

    " Some other persons arrived soon
" after, and my neighbours relinquished to
" them their places, after having spread
" their cloaks under the trees for them to
" repose on. My new companions ordered
" the former to retire, and I found myself
" within hearing of a conversation far more
" interesting than the preceding one, and

" which indeed so engaged my attention,
" that I was on the point of betraying my-
" self.

" I learned, that they had formed the
" design of surprising the count of Wirtem-
" berg at Wisbaden, where he believed him-
" self in security. One of them, whom I
" judged from his discourse to be the com-
" mander of a numerous band, frankly con-
" fessed, that he was not tempted, like his
" followers, by the hope of the immense
" booty they must infallibly gain; but that
" all his desires centered in the beauteous
" wife of count Everard, by whom he had
" formerly been beloved, and who, in a fit
" of disgust, had since given her hand to
" the count.

" My attention was every moment more
" and more excited; for one calculated the
" number of count Everard's enemies, while
" another recited their names amongst
" which were two of the house of Unna,
" the father and the brother of Herman.
" When the dawn began to peep, a greater

" number appeared, and a council was
" held. Two of them related what they
" had observed at Wisbaden: the day of
" attack was fixed, and, and, to my distrac-
" tion, it was the day that was then ap-
" proaching. Instantly I formed the reso-
" lution of warning the count of his dan-
" ger; but to enable him to escape not a
" moment was to be lost.

" Without allowing myself farther time
" for recollection, I rose gently, resolving
" to avail myself of the error into which the
" servants had fallen respecting me, and of
" which I had perceived some traces in the
" conversation of their masters. I turned
" my coat, that it's red lining might appear
" the more terrible, and slowly stalked across
" a path, that led close by them. I found
" that they perceived me, notwithstanding
" the gloom of the wood, and that my ap-
" pearance occasioned a general alarm.—
" They were all at once dumb, as if struck
" with thunder, and I was at some distance
" when I heard the following words, ' It is

" almost day, and yet there is the spectre
" gone by! he is in red too; an omen that
" can bode no good: we shall certainly have
" a bloody day.'

" As soon as I was out of their sight, I
" quickened my pace, and arrived almost
" breathless at Wisbaden. I demanded to
" speak to the count. The persons in
" waiting were astonished to see me, and
" ran instantly to tell him, that Munster,
" who was supposed to be in Italy, was ar-
" rived, and announced his having some-
" thing of importance to communicate.

" I was well received by the count,
" though I had returned without his per-
" mission. Well knowing my fidelity, he
" presumed, that I had not quitted my post
" without reason. I spoke not therefore,
" of the real motives of my journey, but
" instantly disclosed the plot I had over-
" heard in the forest from the knights of
" St. Martin (a name they assumed from
" having formed their design on the eve of

VOL. II.   E

" that, faint), and the moment when they
" intended to put it into execution.

" Unfortunately I related also what the
" discarded lover of the countess of Wir-
" temberg had said of his former intimacy
" with her: and the countess was present.
" She pretended, that I insulted her, and
" that my whole story was a falsehood fa-
" bricated for some ill design; declaring,
" that she had not been ignorant of my ar-
" rival, notwithstanding all my precautions
" to keep it secret; that several of her peo-
" ple had seen me for some days roaming
" about the neighbourhood, and adding
" many other complaints of a similar na-
" ture, which so prejudiced the count
" against all I could say, that he gave or-
" ders for my being imprisoned.

" Conceive what must have been my
" situation. Not only was I suspected by
" my master, and punished for having ful-
" filled the duty of a faithful subject, but
" I beheld the count himself, through his
" own fault, exposed to the most immi-

" nent danger, and with him my Maria,
" and the dear infant whom she loved more
" than life.

" The hour of attack arrived. My
" heart audibly palpitated within me. Yet
" I received a sort of consolation, when I
" heard in the court of the castle the sound
" of horses and carriages, and the clamour
" of the people who seemed eager to go
" out : for I then supposed my information
" had not been wholly disregarded, and
" that it was still possible the object of my
" love might be saved.

" To this tumult a profound silence suc-
" ceeded, that strengthened my hopes, and
" rendered me more tranquil : but soon
" the clashing of arms and neighing of
" steeds informed me, that the knights of
" St. Martin were engaged in their at-
" tempt.

" I was perfectly ignorant of what passed, except that I could hear the groans of
" the dying, and the shouts of the victors,
" when, on a sudden, some words, that con-

E 2

" fusedly struck my ears, led me to sup-
" pose, that the conquerors were resolved
" to crown their enterprize, by committing
" the castle to the flames. The threat
" chilled my blood; and my senses pre-
" sently told me, that it was actually car-
" ried into execution. The smoke entered
" the little grated window of my dungeon,
" which was illuminated by the light of the
" conflagration. A prisoner, I was left to
" perish without succour, unless some
" miracle should come to my deliverance.

" Not conceiving myself sufficiently
" favoured by Heaven to expect such an
" event, I tried the strength of my own
" shoulders in bursting the door of my pri-
" son, and succeeded. Traversing the sub-
" terraneous passage that led to it, I reach-
" ed one of the courts of the castle. One
" wing was entirely in flames; my eyes
" mechanically turned to the other, in
" which was the apartment of Maria. This
" too the flames had already caught in se-
" veral places.——' Fortunately,' said I

" within myself, ' she is safe: for there
" can be no doubt she was amongst those,
" who fled in time from the danger. But
" has she actually escaped? added I, as if
" by secret inspiration! and without fur-
" ther reflection I flew to the place, which
" I had never before visited with similar
" feelings, hoping not to find in it my
" Maria.

" In fact, that part of the castle was
" sufficiently quiet; I saw nobody; but the
" smoke and the heat was scarcely support-
" able. ' Surely Maria cannot be here
" alone, when all the rest of the family
" have escaped,' whispered the desire of
" self-preservation, roused by the danger
" that threatened me at every step: but
" love spoke in a louder tone, boldly urg-
" ing me on in despite of peril; and love
" was victorious. I was determined to be
" convinced by my own eyes, and I
" hastened to ascend the hundred steps,
" that led to the miserable apartment of
" my mistress. As I drew near, I heard

E 3

" the plaintive cries of an infant. I re-
" doubled my speed, and soon distinguished
" the voice of the little Ida. Arrived at
" the door . . . . distraction! it was fasten-
" ed within. The bolts, however, gave
" way to my exertions, and I found Maria
" extended senseless on the floor. The
" window, at which no doubt she had at-
" tempted to escape, but had been terrified
" by its height, was open, and the child had
" crawled along the floor to her nurse,
" whom she endeavoured to awake with
" crying. What a spectacle! . . . But I
" stopped not long to contemplate it. I
" threw Maria across my shoulders, took
" the infant in my arms, and having thus
" gained the court in safety, I set down my
" burden to take breath. It seemed as if
" an angel had lent me wings, so difficult
" did it appear, without supernatural assist-
" ance, to have passed unhurt through
" those volumes of flame and of smoke,
" that on all sides surrounded me.

" Maria coming to herself, we seized
" the first moment of her being able to
" walk to remove from this place of terror;
" for, large as was the court, we were far
" from being in safety there. We soon
" gained the forest, to which, the night be-
" fore, these incendiary banditti had re-
" sorted, and there we ventured to take a
" little rest, believing ourselves secure from
" the fire and sword of the enemy.

" I asked Maria how it had been pos-
" sible for her and the young princess to
" have been thus cruelly abandoned. By
" her answers I found, that she knew no-
" thing of what had passed; that the sight
" of the flames alone had informed her of
" the danger that threatened her life; that
" she had in vain called for assistance, beg-
" ging the door might be opened; that she
" had attempted to leap out of the window;
" and, that, at length, finding herself lost
" without resource, she had swooned with
" despair.

E 4

" It was not till afterwards that I learnt
" the true circumstances of the affair. Count
" Everard, deceived by his wife, God knows
" with what view, gave no credit to my in-
" formation till some hours after my im-
" prisonment. It was then confirmed by a
" neighbouring shepherd, who, as well as I,
" had discovered the project of the knights
" of St. Martin, and hastened to inform
" the count. He then lost not a moment
" in endeavouring to place his family in
" safety, while he determined himself to
" remain in his castle, assemble his men,
" and wait the approach of, the enemy.
" The shepherd offered himself as a guide to
" the fugitives, and to conduct them, by a
" secret road, over the hills. The count,
" as he hastily took leave of his wife, or-
" dered her to take with her every thing
" that was worth carrying off, and repaired
" immediately to his post. The countess
" obeyed her husband's injunctions; she
" left behind her nothing she thought worthy
" her care; the little Ida was forgotten by

" mistake, or perhaps by design; a circum-
" stance not to be wondered at, if we con-
" sider the sentiments and feelings of this
" cruel step-mother.

" Of all this, however, Maria was igno-
" rant. She remarked, indeed, that there
" was a bustle in the court, into which her
" window looked, and preparations making
" for a journey, but she supposed it to be
" nothing more than one of those visits,
" that were occasionally paid to the gen-
" tlemens' seats in the neighbourhood;
" during which she and her charge always
" enjoyed greater liberty, and which, of
" course, she beheld with sensations of plea-
" sure. Besides, the height of her apart-
" ment was too great to suffer her to hear
" what was said below; as was the court too
" distant from the principal front of the
" castle, for her to perceive the attack of
" the enemy.

" The little she heard, however, ren-
" dered her sufficiently curious to endea-
" vour to get out of the prison allotted for

E 5

" her residence; but she found the door
" fastened; at this she was by no means
" surprised, as it frequently happened when
" the countess was in an ill humour. She
" waited therefore, hoping that the girl,
" who usually brought her supper, would
" tell her what was going forward. The
" girl did not make her appearance: it grew
" late: Maria and the little Ida, to whom
" it had before happened more than once
" to go to bed supperless, fell asleep, and
" were at length awakened by the fire. In
" vain she sought to escape; despair and
" terror bereft her of all sensation; and
" when she awoke from her swoon, she saw
" herself saved, saved by me, without
" knowing the occasion of the danger she
" had run, or the manner in which she had
" been extricated from it.

" After having entered into a full ex-
" planation of all these subjects, we began
" to form schemes for our future conduct.
" Mine were totally repugnant to those of
" Maria. I insisted on Ida's being re-

" stored to her father, while she, exasper-
" ated at the barbarity with which the
" poor child had been deserted, swore,
" that she would never more have inter-
" course with me, if I persisted in my de-
" sign.

" To those, who do me the honour to
" listen to my narrative, I leave it to be
" decided, whether, as Maria declared to
" me, to deliver the young princess into
" the hands of her step-mother, and to de-
" prive her of life, would not be one and
" the same thing. For my own part, I was
" then of a different opinion. I confided
" in count Everard's affection for his
" daughter, and hoped, that he would be-
" come a more active protector of her
" helpless infancy, when his eyes were
" opened to the perfidious designs of his
" wife. Necessity, however, conspired
" with love, to prevent the performance
" of what appeared to me so just. I could
" not bear the thoughts of renouncing
" Maria; and to join count Everard, and

" restore to him his daughter, was for the
" present impracticable. The knights of
" St. Martin so infested the roads, that
" every passage was intercepted; and the
" animosity of the imperial towns for a
" long time prevented the count of Wir-
" temberg from having any settled abode.
" He had great difficulty to recover his wife
" from the hands of his enemies, into
" which she had fallen, notwithſtanding the
" precaution that had been employed. At
" length the bishop of Strasburg afforded
" them an asylum; but, being a relation
" of the countess, we were afraid of en-
" trusting Ida to his care.

" Our residence in the forest was of
" short duration, and the first place to
" which we repaired was Nuremberg. The
" loquacity of Maria, quickly discovered
" that we were fugitive and alienated vassals
" of the court of Wirtemberg, and we were
" accordingly received with civility and
" even with kindness. Here I espoused
" her, having, however, been previously

" obliged, before I could obtain her con-
",sent, to bind myself by an oath, not to
" restore Ida to her parents till she should
" be ten years of age, and in the
" mean time to let her pass for my daugh-
" ter. I immediately resumed the profes-
" sion of a sculptor, to which I had been
" bred. Some pieces which I executed
" were considerably admired and gained
" me reputation. I was chiefly employed
" in decorating churches and convents. At
" length I was invited to Prague, where the
" construction of the cathedral detained me
" so long, that I became attached to the
" city, where I had reaped considerable
" emoluments, and I determined to make
" it my future abode. Meanwhile Ida
" grew up. Her beauty, and an education
" which we gave her suitable to her birth,
" occasioned her to be noticed, so that we
" could not admit her to appear in public.
" Once however, my imprudent wife urg-
" ed me to depart from the rule of conduct
" I had laid down, and our supposed daugh-

" ter made her appearance at your majesty's
" nuptials; a step, young princess, that
" proved the source of all the misfortunes
" which has since befallen you."

" Say rather of all my felicity," cried
Ida, tenderly pressing the hand of Sophia
to her lips

" My wife," continued Munster, " had
" her schemes. She was continually re-
" proaching herself for having deprived
" her dear princess of the advantages of
" her birth, and yet was far from consent-
" ing that I should restore her to her father.
" She was in reality desirous of raising her
" to distinction, and obtaining her a for-
" tune, without the succour of the count.
" She could not forgive his blind attachment
" to his second wife, and consequent neg-
" lect of his child, and she therefore hated
" him, too cordially to consent that he
" should have the pleasure of contributing
" to the future happiness of Ida. The
" hopes of my wife were chiefly grounded
" on the favour of the empress; and she

" felicitated herself on the passion for Ida,
" which she soon discovered in the young
" Herman of Unna, and seconded it the
" more readily, because she knew that he
" was an object of enmity to the count of
" Wirtemberg. She formed a thousand
" projects, commited a thousand indiscre-
" tions, till at length she so involved in
" difficulties her, whom she was endea-
" vouring to render happy, that she was on
" the point of falling a victim to her ill-ad-
" vised measures, when I happily interpos-
" ed, and took perhaps the only step that
" could have saved her. I discovered her
" birth to her father. There was no diffi-
" culty in convincing him of the fact; her
" features, and the marks she had brought
" into the world with her, being too well
" known to him to permit him to doubt.—
" His wife had been dead above a twelve-
" month; and, having lately lost the only
" daughter that he supposed remained to
" him, and who had been betrothed to the
" duke of Brunswic, he was not displeased

" at thus unexpectedly finding another.—
" Thus the heart of count Wirtemberg was
" sufficiently at liberty for him to see with
" pleasure, her whom. he had formerly
" abandoned, whom he believed to be dead,
" or at least for ever lost to him, and to
" whom he has just vowed, that every trace
" of what she has suffered, shall be oblite-
" rated by his kindness."

Here Munster closed his recital. Ida
sighed, and Sophia promised to act the part
of a parent to her, and take her under her
under her immediate care, should the count
prove unfaithful to his word. " The point
" most important at present," added she,
" is to devise, my dear friend, the means of-
" expediting your union with Herman.—
" Life is short; we cannot begin too soon
" to be happy. Fathers are often caprici-
" ous. They conceive that they consult.
" sufficiently the happiness of their chil-
" dren, by marrying them to great lords,.
" who possess neither love, nor virtue, nor.
" accomplishments, and whose sole merit is.

" their rank. Ah! Ida, I know more in-
" stances than one of such alliances!"

As she said this, a profound sigh escaped her, which her friend knew perfectly
how to interpret. Ida thanked her for the
interest she took in her welfare, and en-
treated her to attempt nothing in her favour
at present, but to wait rather the operation
of time, which frequently brought things
to pass, that, in prospect, appeared impracticable: a reflection dictated by prudence, which however, Sophia quickly
forgot.

CHAPTER V.

IDA took leave of the empress; and
Munster, to whom she was fond of paying
every mark of respect, having nothing so
much at heart as to display to the world that
she still retained for him a filial regard, and
was not ashamed of having been reputed
his daughter—Munster, I say, accompanied
her home, where they spent together some
delightful hours in conversation. The old
man's narrative had excited in her breast
the liveliest gratitude. The variety of
dangers from which he had extricated her;
the affection, more than parental, with
which he had received her, when abandoned
by every human being; the uniform disin-
terestedness with which he had ever preferred her welfare to his own;—what subjects
of reflection to a heart glowing like her's
with sensibility! At his request however,
she put some little restraint upon herself in
public, but, alone with him, she gave vent

to her feelings, and let loose all the tenderness of her soul.

In their present interview, hours had glided away unperceived, and to finish what they had to say would have required as many more; for the princess took this opportunity of disclosing to Munster the desire she felt of having constantly near her the person whom she had so long called by the endearing name of mother, and to whom she owed such great obligations: a desire with which, she had no doubt, the count of Wirtemberg would readily comply.

Munster shook his head: he seemed neither to desire nor to hope this honour for his wife; and he was about to assign his reasons, when the arrival of the count was announced. Immediately they both rose to meet him. He entered in visible agitation; his countenance portended a storm. He received the caresses of Ida with coldness, and made a sign to her venerable old friend to withdraw.

" I am astonished," said he, after having walked for some time up and down the
room, " I am astonished that you have not
" yet forgotten the past events of your life.
" You are no v the daughter of the count of
" Wirtemberg, and not of that plebeian,
" whom, instead of loading with favour,
" instead of suffering to be in your apart-
" ment for hours together, and of attend-
" ing you in public, you ought to shun
" and detest for the injury he has done
" you."

" What, my father! shun, detest, so
" faithful a servant, the saviour, the protec-
" tor of your daughter, when . . . ."

" He has related to you, it seems, in the
" presence of the empress, the manner in
" which, like a thief, he stole you from me.
" And can you avoid perceiving the baseness
" of the deed? or are you blinded by the
" subterfuges he has invented to excuse
" himself; subterfuges that even were they
" true, would be no justification? It is in

" my, power to punish him; but I would
" gladly wave the exercise of this power in
" consideration of you. Let this content
" you; and urge me not by your conduct
" to extremities.

Ida little accustomed to such remonstrances from a parent, knew not what answer to make and was silent; while her father continued to walk backwards and forwards, in manifest displeasure, till at length
he thus resumed his discourse.

" I have suffered to day in more ways
" than one on your account. In the morn-
" ing I heard of things, that appeared to
" me incredible; and this evening, at court
" I have been told of a circumstance which
" leads me to doubt the purity of thy heart,
" and which if true . . . . . ."

The aspect of the count began to be terrible. Ida interrupted him. " My father,
" my dear father," said she, " look not thus
" sternly on your child! is it possible she
" can have been so unfortunate as to have

" occasioned you uneasiness as to have
" offended you."

    " Yes, if she cannot answer me in the
" negative the questions I shall put to her.
" Is it true that the night I was first known
" to thee as thy father, the night when I
" found thee already risen and dressed at so
" early an hour, is it true that thou hadst
" then a young man with thee, who, on
" my appearance, leaped from the balcony
" into the garden, and that that young man
" was Herman of Unna?—Thou art silent
" —Thou canst not justify thyself?—It is
" then so—But I have another question.—
" To whom am I indebted for the intreaties
" and importunities with which the em-
" press has just been tormenting me upon
" the subject of the love that exists between
" thee and Herman, that shoot of an ac-
" cursed stock ?—Is it possible that my
" daughter, knowing, as she does, that the
" entreaties of sovereigns are commands,
" can have involved me in such a dilemma?"

" —What, still silent?—Well then, I know
" thee; and I know also what I have to do;
" thy sentence is pronounced."

The count of Wirtemberg left his
daughter, and left her in a consternation
that nothing could augment, saving the
order she that evening received to prepare
for a journey, reasons of importance re-
quiring, as she was told, that she should
quit the court with speed.

Ida well knew the reasons of this hasty
departure. She saw all her hopes vanish
into air. She regretted having confided in
a person, whose zeal to serve her had ruin-
ed every thing. She repented every step
she had taken, even her love for Herman,
because she perceived that she should thereby render unhappy a father whom she re-
spected, whom she was desirous of pleasing,
and to whose happiness she would have been
glad to contribute. To be separated from
Munster and the empress, who were so
dear to her, and to be ignorant of her own

fate, were melancholy subjects of reflection; yet to these she wholly abandoned herself, without thinking of going to bed, leaving to her women the care of the preparations she had been ordered to make. Accordingly her father, when he came to her the next morning, found her already dressed: a circumstance that, in spite of the redness of her eyes, which betrayed the tears she had shed, proved that she knew how to obey, and that she was of a character sufficiently gentle to yield to whatever might be required of her.

The observation of this induced count Everard to bestow some endearments on his daughter. He assured her that he loved her sincerely, and would make her happy if she could resolve to obey him; in other words, if she would sacrifice to him her dearest wishes, a trifle, that, in his opinion, ought not to be attended with the smallest difficulty.

Ida was conducted to the empress, to take leave of her. The conversation between Sophia and the count was extremely ·cold. Part of her dissatisfaction appeared to fall even on his daughter, for it was not till the end of the visit that Ida received from her one of those tender embraces to which she had been accustomed. " Un-·" grateful girl," said Sophia, " you love " me not! you have not the courage to re-" sist those who would tear you from me! " Say, count Everard, will you carry your " cruelty so far as to deprive me of my " best and dearest friend, should she be " desirous not to quit me?"

The count knew his daughter sufficiently to believe that he could depend on her. He replied, therefore, that if she felt the least disinclination to obey him, she was at liberty to avow it. Ida perfectly understood the answer that was expected from her, and she was incapable of falshood, she said nothing.

Sophia once more embraced her, but with less affection. The count pressed her hand, to teſtify the satisfaction he felt from her conduct, and they withdrew, attended by all the ladies of the empress, whose eyes, in spite of the pains which they took to conceal it, betrayed the pleasure they experienced at the departure of their companion.

CHAPTER VI.

THE princess of Ratibor may be classed among those women, never wanting in a court, who, to amuse their mistress, or gratify their own curiosity, are ever on the hunt for scandal. Ida had long been the object of her particular attention, and it may be presumed, that, when acknowledged for princess of Wirtemberg, this envious dame would not be less eager to watch her steps and blazon her actions. She was acquainted with every circumstance that passed in the most secret retirement of our heroine, and even the noctural visit in the balcony had not escaped her knowledge. She was not absolutely sure that the young man was Herman; but she boldly ventured the conjecture, and thus stumbled by accident on the truth.

She had already several times attempted to injure the reputation of Ida, and de-

F 2

prive her of the empress's esteem; and with the same views she triumphantly related this adventure, embellished with circumstances tending to give it an appearance of criminality: but as Sophia had already been made acquainted with the affair, in the naked simplicity of the truth, she failed in her attempt, and was accordingly obliged to change her battery. It was she who acquainted the count of Wirtemberg with the occurrence, and who dictated to the centinel what answers to make in case he should be examined on the subject. And thus, by her indefatigable zeal, did she at last attain the accomplishment of what she had so much at heart, the removal of the object of her detestation.

Ida remarked indeed, when her father took leave of the princess of Ratibor, that they were on better terms than usual;· but she was too ingenuous to divine the cause; too ingenuous to suspect, (though at the door of the anti-chamber she saw them in earnest conversation,) what, had she known, would have driven her to despair. For the count had requested the princess of Ratibor to watch the proceedings of Herman, who, she said, had been seen in the city so lately as the preceding evening; and to take some means, if he could be laid hold of, of compelling him to renounce Ida for ever.

Count Everard, it is probable, was not aware of all the malignity of her whom he charged with such a commission: for he surely sought not the ruin of Herman, and would perhaps have wished him a long and happy life, provided it was spent at the distance of a hundred leagues from his daughter.

Meanwhile some good genius interfered in the preservation of the young knight.— What the princess of Ratibor had said was true. He was still in the neighbourhood, where he had remained to watch the motions of Ida, and find some opportunity of speaking to her. By his extreme vigilance he learned the departure of his mistress juſt before she stepped into the carriage; and the place having no longer any attractions for him, he instantly quitted it, and thus escaped the dangers by which he was surrounded.

His intention was to follow her wherever she might go, and, under a thousand different disguises, to try if he could not, by some lucky chance, obtain from her a word or a look. This he would probably have executed to their mutual injury, had not Heaven sent him a friend, by whose counsels he was induced to adopt a wiser plan of conduct. Herman, by the means of the little stratagems he employed, had contrived to learn, that Ida and her father were to sleep the second night after their departure at a village with which he was acquainted. To this village he repaired by a shorter way than that usually taken by travellers; and as he waited there for his mistress, hoping at least to enjoy the pleasure of seeing her alight, and of hearing her voice, he was

accosted on a sudden by his old friend
Munster.

Our manuscript does not inform us,
whether this worthy plebeian was actuated
by the same views as the knight of fidelity;
it only says, that he totally reprobated
those of the latter, and employed all the
influence he had over his mind to induce
him to renounce them.—" And what," said
he, after Herman had opened to him his
heart, " will be the fruit of this mad pro-
" ject? To lose your time in a wild-goose
" chase; to remain to eternity a simple
" knight, who can never think of becoming
" the son-in-law of the proud count of Wir-
" temberg; to let flip a thousand oppor-
" tunities of acquiring glory; to endanger
" your life, your honour, and even the
" honour of your mistress, should you
" be discovered; and should you not be
" discovered, to spend whole years in
" useless labours, in order to arrive at an
" end which can never be so attained, and to
" discover, too late, that you have followed

F 4

" the shadow, when you might have made
" giant strides towards happiness. No, sir
" knight, this must not be. Take the ad-
" vice of an old friend, and quit this place;
" quit it instantly, before she who may
" shake your resolution shall arrive. Go,
" resume the office you quitted, when you
" hastened to the succour of Ida. You left
" Sigismond in evil hands. Love hitherto
" may be a sufficient excuse for your con-
" duct; but nothing can justify your longer
" delaying to fulfil the duty you owe to
" your sovereign. Strange rumours are
" current concerning him; if well founded,
" your means of serving him will I fear be
" of little avail; but your fidelity may re-
" animate the hopes of this unfortunate
" prince. Perhaps at this moment you
" are the only person sincerely attached to
" him: and can you have the cruelty to
" abandon him? Would you leave him
" wholly deſtitute of a friend?"

In this manner did the old man endeavour to awaken in the soul of Herman a

love of glory, of duty, and of fidelity to his sovereign; to guard him against a hopeless passion, and to rouse him from the life of indolence, so unworthy of him, to which he was on the point of devoting himself. And he had the satisfaction to see his endeavours crowned with success. Herman vowed to remain eternally faithful to Ida, but promised at the same time that it should not be at the expence of his other duties. Munster, on his part, engaged to watch unremittingly over the young princess, and they took leave of each other sincere and cordial friends.

F 5

CHAPTER VII.

HERMAN departed.   The information given him by Munster of the doubtful situation of Sigismond was confirmed to him on the road.   In one place it was said, that he was yet not returned from the campaign againſt the infidels, and probably had fallen into their hands; in another, that he was in the power of ſtill more dangerous enemies at home; sometimes that he was mortally wounded; then that he was dead.   These rumours however decreased as Herman advanced into Hungary, and totally died away before he reached the capital, where he found that preparations were making with royal magnificence for the reception of his maſter.

As I am not writing the hiſtory of Sigismond, I shall speak of his concerns so far only as they have an immediate relation with the adventures of Herman.   I shall therefore say nothing of the king's entrance into Presburg, where he was receiv'd with loud acclamations by the people, who loved him in spite of his faults: neither shall I notice the crowd of nobles that surround him, or the mutual promises that were made in order to establish a good understanding between them and the monarch. No doubt, the levity, the libertinism, the propensity to drinking, and the occasional cruelty of Sigismond, were sufficient causes of discontent to a considerable number of his subjects; and he had obtained no victory, he had made no conquest, the splendor of which might have thrown these qualities into shade: yet, for some reason or other, the past was promised to be forgotten on both sides, and Sigismond was but too ready to shut his eyes against a thousand marks of disloyalty and treason manifested by the principal lords of his court, and particularly the two Garas.

The numerous guests who were assembled in the place on the evening of the king's arrival, kept Herman, who burned.

with the desire of seeing him, at a distance.
—His situation was embarrassing, and he
knew not how to act.   To his former pa-
tron general Gara, who had found him in-
corruptible in the late campaign against the
Turks, he was an object of detestation ; and
Herman, in his turn, felt no esteem for a
man whom he knew to be the secret enemy
of his master, much less could he bring
himself to ask him a favour.   At length the
young knight determined to be his own in-
troducer.   Accordingly he placed himself
near the king.   Sigismond observed him.
The face of Herman was not of that insipid
and common-place sort which one may
meet twenty times without recollecting a
feature; the king beside, when he last saw
him, was in a situation too critical for him
to forget a single individual of those who
surrounded him, and much less the person
who had been the principal actor.

At first Sigismond had some difficulty in
collecting his ideas. He appeared thought-
ful, rubbed his forehead, and then turning

to Andrew Gara, who was seated by his side: " Whence comes it," said he, " that " often in the midst of our joy and convivi- " ality, melancholy remembrances so sud- " denly assail us? One of the most perilous " events of my life at this moment presents " itself to my eyes. Can you not guess " what I mean? Know you not who that " young man is?"

Andrew bowed, and was silent. " But " perhaps," continued Sigismond, " you " may be ignorant of the transaction ; you " were not present ; it was your brother. " You would not so cowardly have deserted " me. I have promised to forget the " treachery of my enemies, but never will " I forget the services of my friends. I " was, as I have said, cowardly deserted. " Already was my head exposed to the faul- " chion of Achmet, and there was but a " step between me and death, when a troop " of chevaliers came to my deliverance. " My horse had been killed under me ; my " helmet and buckler were hacked to pieces ;

" and I had no weapon but my sabre. The
" leader of this brave troop leaped from
" his horse, gave me his shield, and with
" his own helmet covered my head. What
" happened afterwards I know not, for I
" became insensible to every thing around
" me.   But there remains deeply engraven
" in my mind, the remembrance of my
" deliverer, whose countenance seemed ra-
" diant as that of an angel descended from
" Heaven.   It is that countenance, which
" now recalls to my mind the particulars of
" the horrid scene: I discern it amongst
" the crowd of those who surround my
" table: it displays the features of my loyal
" servant Herman of Unna, so often calum-
" niated.   Draw near, intrepid youth, by
" whom my life has been saved! receive
" the thanks of thy king, and assurance of
" his favour!"

While Sigismond was speaking, Herman
had listened with attention, that he might
not lose a word of what concerned him so
nearly.   When the king had finished, our

hero, transported with joy, fell at his feet, kissed his hand, and bathed his knees with tears. What glory for him, what satisfaction, to be thus praised before a thousand witneſſes by a sovereign, who had always appeared to slight him, and to whom he had given a hundred proofs of attachment, without his seeming to have paid them the least attention!

After these effusions of joy, our young knight modestly retired amongst the gentlemen in waiting; but Sigismond frequently turned to look for him, and at length forbad him to quit his side.

The proud nobles, who were at table with the king, appeared to have taken no part in the scene they witnessed. They kept a profound silence, and deigned not to pay the least compliment to the young warrior, whom Sigismond had so distinguishingly honoured.

Thus he received no congratulations, but from those who waited with him at table, among whom he recognized many an old friend and comrade. But of all the persons he met at this festival, none gave him so much pleasure as a young man, whom he had known when a child, and with whom he had formerly a misunderstanding at the court of Winceslaus. He was in the number of knights attendants of king Sigismond; and as, in the war against the Mussulmen, Herman had seen him act with valour, the remembrance of past wrongs was entirely obliterated in his mind, and replaced by a sincere attachment and esteem. It was Kunzman of Hertingshausen, who had ascribed to Herman, when page to Winceslaus, the necessity he was under of flying from the emperor's court. The reader will no doubt recollect the circumstance, related to Munster by the knight of fidelity, when he gave him the history of his younger years.

Kunzman, who, when he met with Herman in the course of the campaign against the Turks, appeared to have forgotten his ancient enmity, accosted him on this occasion as a real friend. The place was not calculated for a long conversation; a squeeze by the hand, and " my dear " Herman," " my dear Hertingshausen," were all that passed; the rest was postponed to the interview they promised themselves the succeeding night.

The king, engaged for some time in a serious conversation with the two Gara's, had ceased to look after Herman: the guests had drunk largely: it was not the cup of pleasure that circulated round the table, it was the cup of infernal discord. Herman had long observed with pain, that the nobles who sat opposite his master paid him not the respect which was due to him. Grim discontent, or malignant joy, was legible in their countenances, enflamed by the intoxicating wines of Hungary. Much too was he displeased with the discourse which the two brothers directed to the king.— They appeared to have entirely forgotten to whom they were speaking. The subject was the late unfortunate campaign, in which the king was so near losing his life. Reproaches passed on both sides; these reproaches were repelled with mutual warmth; but soon the general and his brother spoke in so loud and lofty a tone, as to drown the single voice of the monarch.

"What!" said Herman to Hertingshausen, putting his hand to his sword, "shall we suffer our master to be thus insulted?" The uproar, increased; all rose from their seats; here and there sabres were drawn, and the king was at length so pressed, that the ill designs harboured against his person were no longer doubtful. Instantly Herman drew his sword, and his example was followed by Hertingshausen, and all the other young knights who were present. Sigismond was thrown down, and his enemies dared employ against him weapons, which to all true knights are prohibited. Upon this Herman seized Andrew Gara by the throat and plucked him forcibly from the body of his master; and others did the same by the general; the king was rescued, and the knights gained the field of battle. But soon the match became too unequal: a considerable body of cavaliers was introduced, and the defenders of Sigismond were soon beaten to the ground, others disarmed, and all, as well as the king, treated with the utmost indignity, and loaded with chains.

Two only however of these had the honour eventually to share his fate, Herman and Hertingshausen. The others, almost all effeminate courtiers, were easily turned from their duty, either by promises, or by threats; and none of them envied the two loyal servants of Sigismond the advantage of participating their master's misfortunes, of being like him ill-treated, fettered, put into a covered waggon, and conducted to a place where the artful nobles hoped they should be able to deal with the king as they pleased, without having any thing to apprehend from the people.

CHAPTER VIII.

THE prisoners were conducted to the castle of Soclos. Herman knew this castle to be the principal seat of the Gara family, and could therefore easily imagine what treatment his unfortunate master had to expect in a place where his enemies enjoyed unlimted power. His expectations, however, which foreboded nothing but insult and death to Sigismond, were for once disappointed.

The event which led to the seizure of the king was by no means accidental, but the result of a previously concerted scheme. It had been resolved to secure his person, dethrone him, and put another in his place: but in the execution of this plan, the line chalked out had been outrageously departed from, and it was presently thought adviseable to assume some appearance of decency and moderation. Intoxication had made the enemies of Sigismond forget, that he whom they thus treated as a vile slave was still their sovereign, and that this disgraceful proceeding would bring public dishonor on themselves. When the fumes of wine therefore had somewhat evaporated, though the Garas did not less burn with the desire of vengeance than before, they were ashamed to persevere in a conduct, that might ruin their pretensions to the crown of Hungary, and induce the people to take the part of the contemptible son of Charles IV.

The king's fetters were accordingly taken off; and, from the dungeon to which he had at first been consigned, he was transferred to a splendid apartment: he was even asked, if he wished to be waited on by those gentlemen of his court, who were prisoners with him; and, on his answering in the affirmative, they were enlarged for that purpose.

The situation of Sigismond was now supportable; and it became still more so, when Nicholas and Andrew, the two Garas, obliged to quit the castle on account of

some affairs, that required their attendance
at the capital, relinquished to their mother-
in-law the care of the royal prisoner.

Before I proceed with my narrative, it
may not be amiss to give the reader some
account of this lady, Helen Gara, widow
of the deceased Nicholas, whom Sigismond
had formerly put to death, and step-mother
to the general and the governor. She was
a young and handsome widow of twenty-
five, who had not been so inconsolable at
the loss of her old and decrepid husband,
as to retain any very durable hatred against
his murderer. It is true she had talked of
nothing but vengeance as long as her sons-
in-law were within hearing, and appeared
to enter into their views, because she found
it necessary to the compassing her own:
but the imprisonment of Sigismond in the
castle of Soclos, inspired her with designs
very different from those entertained by his
enemies.

The love of pleasure and the love of
sway constituted the grand features of her

character. Sigismond, notwithstanding his
age, was one of the handsomest princes of
his time; he was a king, he was brother
to the emperor, and would in all probability
succeed him, if Winceslaus should die or
be dethroned. What subjects for reflection; what allurements to a woman such as
we have described the mistress of the
castle! Could she hesitate? could she remain in doubt, whether to favour the unjust
designs of her sons-in-law, the accomplishment of which might probably be remote,
even did they ever succeed, or to ingratiate
herself with a prince, who might repay her
kindness by instantly sharing with her his
bed and his throne?

In imagination Helen already saw herself the wife of Sigismond, and swaying
with him the first sceptre in the world: nor
was she tardy in taking such steps, as she
deemed most conducive to the attainment
of her wishes. She enjoyed the perfect confidence of both her step-sons: she knew

that they would be some time absent, endeavouring to place the crown on the head of young Ladislaus: and she hastened to execute the projects she had formed.

The king had one whole wing of the castle appropriated to his use. His court, hitherto composed solely of Kunsman and Herman of Unna, was now augmented.— He was treated as a sovereign, had permission to walk in the gardens, and there was nothing to remind him of his being a prisoner, but the guards that always accompanied, at a certain distance, him and his two gentlemen.

Sigismond rejoiced at this change in his lot, which elated him with hope. He sought to develope the cause; and he was not long in discovering, that it originated in the benevolence of the princess. The portrait of Helen decorated all his apartments, and he had sometimes seen the original, at a distance in the garden, not without admiration.

There was no snare so dangerous to Sigismond, as female beauty. Whilst, however, he paid homage to its charms, he had
too high an opinion of himself to think any
woman could resist him. With the sentiments of Helen he was soon acquainted;
her action spoke a language sufficiently
plain. His love of ease, and the suscepti-
bility of his heart, were daily flattered by .
new attentions; and his gratitude, his inclination for the fair enchantress, who had
the art of rendering his prison so agreeable,
were heightened by her having the address
to avoid him, and give him no opportunity
of thanking her in person. The view of her
portrait, and the praises continually bestowed on her by those about him, trans-
formed his gratitude into the most violent
love. He burned with the desire of seeing her. Secret proposals were then made,
emissaries sent from one to the other, and
meetings took place, till the parties were
perfectly agreed. Decency led them to endeavour to throw a veil over their proceed-

ings; but the veil was so transparent, that
it left the inmates of the castle little to
divine.

In this affair, Kunzman of Hertingshausen acted the principal part. He displayed
peculiar talents for such negociations, and
completely acquired by it the confidence of
his master.

Herman had no concern in the business;
nor was there a man in the world less proper for the office. He knew but one spe-
cies of love, that which he felt for Ida,
and of which pure hearts alone are susceptible. An amorous intrigue was deemed
by him incompatible with virtue; and he
was not politic enough to conceal the disgust with which it inspired him. When
yet a page in the court of Winceslaus, impudence and libertinism had been seen by
him under all their most odious forms, and
he sincerely regretted, that similar scenes
were about to be renewed here, by a prince
whom he loved, and in whom he discovered
with sorrow, the same proneness to de-

bauchery, as had disgusted him in his imperial brother.

Sigismond, not being accustomed to read in the eyes of those about him, a secret disapprobation of his conduct, Herman was kept at a distance, and the wily messenger of love, the complaisant Hertingshausen, employed on every occasion.

As Herman's attachment to his master had considerably diminished, he was less sensible to the preference given another, and envied not Kunzman the favour of a prince whom he would now willingly have quitted. " To what purpose is the effe-minate life I am leading here?" would he say to himself. " Is this the way to raise " myself to distinction, and render myself " worthy of the princess of Wirtemberg? " Oh! fly, Herman, fly! thou art here wast-" ing thy time in a manner still more re-" prehensible, than that depicted by Mun-" ster, in colours so disadvantageous."

G 2

CHAPTER IX.

EVERY thing has an end: a passion of the nature of that of Helen and Sigismond, is beside seldom of long duration, and we are almost tempted to give the princess some credit for its brevity, by attributing it to her little experience on such subjects. How could she think to fix for ever her lover? How hope, at some future period, to share his throne? Love, and her confidence in her charms, must have certainly blinded her, and she could never have heard of the former adventures of the faithless Sigismond. She had calculated too much on his constancy; and so completely had he subjugated her, that, instead of being a prisoner in the castle of Soclos, he was become in reality its master.

It never entered the mind of Helen, that Sigismond was secretly contriving to deliver himself at once, both from his prison and his mistress, of whom he was now equally weary; and her surprise was extreme, when one day he entered her chamber equipped for a journey. At first she was thunderstruck; but supposing he might be going a hunting, she offered to accompany him. " No, my charming princess," " said Sigismond, " I must leave you."

" Leave me? I am answerable with my " life for your person!"

" And is mine in no danger, if I re- " main longer here? Your rebellious sons " are informed of the kindness with which " you treat me : they will soon arrive, and " will load me with chains, somewhat " heavier than those in which you have " held me captive."

" Alas! I perceive they are too light; " you will easily shake them off."

" Dear-Helen! is it possible for me in " this place, in the arms of love, to take " the necessary steps to regain the throne, " from which I have been hurled? Think " what you require! Think of the happi- " ness, the reputation of him whom you " love!"

G 3

Helen fell into a profound reverie, from which at length she recovered to ask, " whether, if fortune favoured him, he would still think of her, and would not forget the love and constancy he had sworn ?"

Sigismond, who gave himself little trouble about the vows he made to a mistress, readily acquiesced, and his language was in other respects so tender, that she was duped by his artifice, and consented to his escape. She then prayed him at least to stay a few days longer before he left her. The king was all compliance; but as this delay by no means suited him, and he was apprehensive of losing the opportunity that offered of regaining his liberty, he resolved to escape secretly, which served to justify Helen to her sons from having any concern in his flight.

―――――

CHAPTER X.

NO one was more pleased than Herman at having escaped from the palace of this Circe. He rejoiced, that he was at length emancipated from a life of idleness, without being obliged to quit his master, whom he considered as restored to virtue, and of consequence again began to love. Sigismond bent his course to the castle of count Cyly, the brother of his sister's husband, where adventures awaited him, that deprived him anew of the heart of the loyal knight of Unna.

The Cylys had always been partisans of Sigismond. One was bound to him by family ties; the other, count Peter Cyly, at whose house he was now a guest, was linked to his fate by a still more powerful charm. This Peter was surnamed the Weak, an appellation he well deserved, and had nothing to recommend him but his wife, the hand-

G 5

some Barbe, formerly maid of honour to queen Mary of Hungary, and for whom he was indebted to Sigismond. Barbe was the guarantee of her husband's fidelity, as, but for her, he might easily have been gained by any one that knew his imbecility. She was entirely devoted to the king, profeffedly from gratitude for having bestowed her on Peter the Weak; her spouse, at least, was fully convinced of this; but there were people who thought differently, and the sequel will probably inform us, which party was in the right. Thus much is certain, that Barbe had maintained the best disposition of loyalty towards Sigismond in her husband, who had always need of being moved by some external impulse, to enable him to take part in any thing; and that she was the principal motive, that had induced the king to prefer the castle of count Peter for his asylum. Sigismond and his two companions, Herman and Hertingshausen, were received with open arms; and though the count expressed simply enough his a to-nishment at this sudden visit, it appeared, nevertheless, that Barbe had long expected her illustrious guest.

Herman was not so blind on the subject as count Cyly. He observed looks of intelligence between his master and the countess; he perceived also, that Hertingshausen was at the bottom of the secret, and treated by Barbe as an old acquaintance. Hence it was easy for him to infer, that the frequent absence of Hertingshausen, during the latter part of their abode at the castle of Soclos, when Sigismond and his people were no longer treated as prisoners, was for the purpose of carrying on a secret correspondence between the king and the countess; and that his master had been prompted to quit Helen; less from disgust of the idle and voluptuous life he led with her, than a desire to visit his ancient friend.

A few days was sufficient to convince Herman, that the scenes of dissipation which had taken place in the castle of Soclos would here be renewed; and that his hopes

G 5

of re-entering on an active life, and of pursuing his fortune, were built on a sandy foundation.

This conviction led him to resume his former purpose of leaving his master, as, there was nothing to induce him to stay at the castle of Cyly.   It is true, that it was sometimes proposed in the cabinet council of Sigismond, to take effective measures for replacing the monarch immediately on the throne; but these measures were deferred from day to day, and the means chosen for the accomplishment of this great design consisted less in the employment of force of arms, than of artifice and intrigue; things in which Herman was totally unskilled, and of which he was even so impolitic as to own his disapprobation.

What rendered his abode at the castle of Cyly still more disagreeable was the want of a friend, whom he could love, and in whom he might confide.   Before they left Soclos, the conduct of Hertingshausen had more than once excited his contempt, and here it soon rendered him totally unworthy the affection of a man like Herman. Hertingshausen did not content himself with being the go-between of an illicit amour, he sought also to participate in the pleasures of his master. He had eyes only for the handsome countess, and the countess put no restraint on her's, unless when in danger of being observed by Sigismond. With respect to our knight, whom she had considered from the beginning as a personage of no consequence, she feared not his notice, and was as little reserved before him as before her blind and imbecile husband. Indeed so excessive was the impudence of the countess, that the innocence and purity of Herman's mind would scarcely permit him to credit the testimony of his senses. Meanwhile he knew not yet how far this new Meſſalina could carry her effrontery and licentiousness, of which history has transmitted to us some account; nor was he fully convinced, till at length she cast her lascivious eyes upon him with intent to draw him also into her snares.

I shall here drop the curtain, to conceal
from my reader the horrible scenes that
passed in the castle of Cyly; and content
myself with saying, that they were such,
as, in the eyes of Herman, to give it the
appearance of an infernal abode, which he
thought continually of quitting; and that
the only circumstance, by which he was detained, was his being doubtful whether he
ought to be silent, before he departed, or
inform his master of the abominable practices of the countess.   The former his pro-
bity forbad; and his delicacy revolted at
the latter.

In the explanation that he must have
entered into with Sigismond, he must have
owned his knowledge of the monarch's con-
nections with the wife of count Peter, and
that, perhaps, without daring to have expressed all the horror with which it inspired
him; a conduct which appeared to him a
sort of tacit approbation, to which he could
by no means bring himself to consent: and
thus he remained undecided, till new dis-

coveries filled up the measure of his indignation, and precipitated his departure.

The contempt with which Herman repaid the advances of the countess had drawn
on him her hatred, nor was she contented
till she had infused similar sentiments into
the mind of Sigismond. Hertingshausen
had already, at Soclos, deprived Herman of
the first place in his master's affections; and
at Cyly our knight ceased to be summoned
to the deliberations held on the subject of
reinstating Sigismond on the throne. He
discovered too, that the regaining of the
crown of Hungary was not the sole object
in agitation; for the ambitious Barbe had
inspired the king with more elevated pretensions. It had formerly been predicted
to her, that she should be an empress; already she considered herself as the wife of
Sigismond; and it is therefore not to be
wondered at, that she sought to instil into
him the desire of ascending the imperial
throne, the object of her dearest wishes, and

to which she had no hope of arriving, unless he was seated upon it himself.

All these things gave infinite displeasure to Herman. He heard of plots forming against the life not only of Winceslaus, whose crown already tottered on his head, but also of duke Frederic of Brunswick, and other nobles, who had pretensions to the imperial sceptre; and he dreaded, lest he should not arrive in time to caution and to save them. In this emergency, Herman had the generosity to forget, that duke Frederic was his rival designed by the count of Wirtemberg to become the consort of Ida: he considered him only as a prince threatened with cowardly assasination, for whose safety, as well as that of Winceslaus, he would readily, on such an occasion, have sacrificed his existence.

Herman was now unalterably determined to quit, without delay, this den of murderers. But it was not so easy as he thought to escape from the castle of Cyly. A lofty wall surrounded the park through which it

was necessary to pass. To this wall there
was but one gate, which shut by night, and
strictly guarded by day. Thus he discovered, that Sigismond and his people were
no less prisoners here than in the castle of
Soclos. At first Herman had fixed on the
night for the execution of his design: but
he was obliged to change his purpose, and
wait for day; flattering himself, that he
could effect his escape more easily by means
of a present to the guard, than by endeavouring, with his single strength, to burst
enormous gates fortified with bars of iron.
With this view he went to repose himself
in one of those delightful alcoves or shrub-
beries, with which the park abounded, and
there was witness to a conversation, that we
think of sufficient importance to be com-
municated to the reader in a chapter by
itself.

CHAPTER XI.

HERMAN presently perceived that he was not alone in the alcove. His safety required that he should not be discovered, and thus necessity obliged him for once to play the eaves-dropper, in spite of the contempt he had always entertained for so despicable a practice. The reader will learn who were the persons that preceded our hero from the following conversation, to which his arrival gave birth.

" Hark! I hear a noise."

" It is nobody, countess: it is only the " rustling of the leaves."

" I would not for the world any one " should overhear us.

" It is impossible; your two husbands, " as you have seen, are dead drunk."

" My *two* husbands, indeed! A pretty " conceit! You are jealous, Hertingshausen?"

" It is for husbands to be jealous of the " lover, not a happy lover of the husband."

" And jealous they will be. Ah, Kunz-
" man! Another time let me beseech you
" to be more prudent; to-night you quite
" forgot yourself. Be contented with giv-
" ing me proofs of your affection when we
" are alone: but in presence of the king,
" before count Peter . . . Surely the wine
" must have deranged your intellects."

" You are alarmed without cause. Si-
" gismond and the count were both scarce-
" ly capable either of seeing or hearing."

" But know you not, that, in their cups,
" fools become wise and cowards brave."

" Brave indeed! I would not have ad-
" vised him, when sober, to strike me for
" stealing a kiss from your lips."

" Fie, Kunzman! You would have borne
" it, and I cannot help thinking of the dis-
" grace you have sustained, Leave me.—
" I will never suffer by my side a man
" whom Peter the Weak has beaten."

" Countess!"

" You are yet but a simple page.—
" Leave me, I say. Herman for me! He

" would not have taken a blow from count
" Peter, nor even from king Sigismond
" himself.

" Herman, countess! Do not render me
" desperate! You know what I have already
" said on this cursed subject.   Is it not true,
" that, had he been as willing as yourself,
" you would have made him happy?"

" The brave are always happy."

" Heavens! I shall go distracted! . . . .
" Herman, Herman! Where art thou?
" Where shall I find thee? Thy doom is
" fixed."

" This might be well in a man who had
" no fears. However, to-morrow count
" Peter is to hunt with the brave Herman.
" If you have any inclination, you may
" avenge yourself of both at once. Go:
" let us see with what deeds of heroism,
" love and vengeance will inspire you. But,
" to speak frankly, you will return, I have
" no doubt, with your hands and garments
" as spotless as they are at this moment.
" How indeed should it be possible to defile

" with blood those pretty white fingers, or
" that spruce silk doublet!"

The discourse of this fury was more than
once interrupted by the blasphemies of the
enraged Hertingshausen; and when it was
finished, he rushed like lightning from the
alcove, while Barbe burst into an infernal
laugh, loud enough to reach his ears notwithstanding his speed.

Herman was so astonished at what he had
heard, that he knew not how he ought to
act. The conclusion of the countess's
speech would have induced him to make his
escape, had not a sentiment of honour withheld him. He had never been accustomed
to fly before his enemies; and, beside, he
trembled for the life of the count, with whom
he was in reality engaged to hunt the next
day. From the extreme imbecility of his
understanding, Herman was induced to consider him in the light of a woman, and consequently deemed himself bound as a loyal
knight to protect him from outrage.

He was detained a few minutes longer
in the alcove by the arrival of Barbe's waiting maid.

"Retire, lovers!" said she: "day be-
"gins to dawn."

"Your caution is useless," answered
Barbe: "I am alone."

"Alone!"

"I have at length roused Hertingshau-
"sen out of his lethargy. Neither Herman
"nor Peter will survive the approaching
"day: I have set a famished tiger at their
"heels. I know Kunzman; he will cer-
"tainly put them to death, let him find
"them where he will."

"But why? good God! why?"

"Fool, that thou art! Every day am I
"not exposed to the contemptuous looks of
"the one, and thou knowest how the other
"behaved last night. I wanted only to see
"my lover struck by my stupid husband:
"it will next be my turn."

"And shall I be able after this, my
"lady, to say that you are not cruel?"

" Cruel!—For the tenth time let me
" remind thee of queen Mary. Does she
" not still live peaceably in her convent?
" Have I not disdained to spill her blood,
" though it would secure my fortune?"

The sequel will perhaps inform us, whether Herman comprehended these words, or
reflected seriously on their meaning. But
the haste with which he quitted the alcove,
as they were uttered, leaves room to doubt
his having heard them.

" What is that!" exclaimed the maid,
whom Herman had jostled, as he passed
between her and the branches of the alcove.

" Good God!" cried Barbe: " If any
" one has over heard us!"

" Just as you were speaking of the
" queen, something passed me so quickly
" .... Ah, madam! I tremble I
" fear .... Is it indeed true, that your
" hands are not stained with the queen's
" blood?"

" I swear they are, not . . . . Why should
" I assassinate a rival, who injures me so
" little with Sigismond? I never shed blood
" out of wantonness."

" It is very cold, madam ; besides, it
" is almost day; will you please to go
" in ?"

Barbe was silent ; and they quitted the
alcove.

CHAPTER XII.

IN vain did Herman traverse the forest in quest of his adversary. Not being able to find him he hastened back to the castle, to inform count Peter of his danger. He too had disappeared; Hertingshausen, it was said, had come for him from king Sigismond half an hour before, and Herman had also been inquired after.

Herman could guess; at least pretty nearly, the road Kunzman was likely to take with the unfortunate count. It was not difficult for so artful a traitor to carry the feeble minded Peter wherever he could with most security execute his detestable purpose. The defender of the unhappy victim quickened his steps, but scarcely had he quitted the castle when he beheld himself surrounded by the guards, who demanded his sword in the name of king Sigismond, and told him that they must conduct him instantly to prison.

Herman obeyed, or rather was forced to obey. Resitance would have been useless; its only consequence would have been the shedding of innocent blood, without perhaps effecting his escape. He was shut up in a tower in the north wing of the castle; on his asking his conductors what was his crime, they shrugged up their shoulders but gave him no answer; they promised, however, at his urgent intreaties, to send to the forest in search of count Peter, who he assured them was in danger of his life.

Towards noon the prisoner was conducted before his judge. King Sigismond cast on him, for the first time in his life, a look of indignation. Herman stood before him with that air of confidence which innocence alone can give.

" Vile, dissembling hypocrite!" exclaimed the king: " was it for thee to take " upon thyself the character of a preacher " of virtue, to censure, with so envious an " eye, innocent pleasures, whilst at the

" same time thou wert secretly attempting
" to ravish thy master's property?"

" Let your majesty deign to pardon him,
" in consideration of his youth:" interposed
Erbe, whom Herman had not before
noticed: " Perhaps he had drank too freely,
" and was not in his senses: besides, what
" is a kiss?"

" A kiss!" cried Sigismond: " To you
" indeed, a kiss seems a trifle! Traitress,
" you love Herman, or you would not
" speak thus."

" Have I then been mistaken for Her-
" tingshausen?" asked Herman, casting a
look of contempt on the countess.

" My eyes, it is true, told me that it
" was Hertingshausen," said the king:
" They represented to me, not thy figure
" but his. But I will not believe their
" testimony; I was half asleep, and the coun-
" tess is in the right: it was not he, it was
" thou, who hadst the boldness to attack
" what is most dear to me in the world?'

VOL. II.   H

" My lord! my king!" resumed Barbe,
with a suppliant voice, " You are certainly
" deceived: yes, yes, it was Hertingshausen,
" and not this poor Herman: pardon him,
" pray pardon him, if you would not have
" me die too!"

" Withdraw:" said Sigismond : " The
" kiss shall not cost thee thy life; it is but
" a trifle, as the countess says.   But that
" she loves thee! that the most beautiful of
" her sex adores thee, and would die with
" thee! . . . . Distraction! . . . Retire; re-
" tire from my sight."

Herman was led back to his prison. He
saw what was the design of his accuser. Her
equivocal answers, the inclination she pretended for him, were meant to inflame the
jealousy of Sigismond. She was well aware,
that a look, a tear, would protect her from
the rage of her lover; but she wished Herman to become its victim.

" This was a master stroke," said Barbe
to her waiting woman, when she was alone
with her. " Sigismond saw but too clearly

" in his cups. He would infallibly have
" put Hertingshausen to death. How lucky
" that I was able to make him believe Her-
" man to be the guilty person!"

" Alas! I was so pleased," said the servant, "when I found him here in the court
" of the castle! so happy that he had escaped
" the sword of Kunzman! and now a new
" danger has befallen him. Ah! why did
" I not conceal from you . . . ."

" Weak creature! Surely thou dost not
" weep?"

" And yet you loved him once?"

" Put thyself in my place, and thou
" wilt then conceive, of what slighted love
" is capable."

" I could not hate so noble a youth,
" however he might despise me."

" Hold thy peace, and see if Hertings-
" hausen be not yet coming. He will at
" least have executed one of my com-
" missions."

The maid looked, weeping, out of the
window, as did Herman, at the same mo-

H 2

ment from the grille of his prison, towards the road that led to the forest.

Night was approaching. A troop of horsemen, issuing from the wood, advanced full speed towards the castle. Despair was visible in their eyes, and the words they uttered, as they alighted at the gate, seemed rather confused murmurs, than articulate words. Two of them passed under his grated window, and he heard the following conversation :

" How terribly the boar has gored him " in his side," said one : " I never before " beheld such a wound."

" It was no boar," said the other, " take " my word for it; but the sabre of some " assassin. Sir Herman was right, when " he sent us to his succour : surely he has " the gift of prophecy."

" And there was no life in him ? He " was actually dead ?"

" Alas ! yes . . . . He was a good mas- " ter; he never did injury to any one.— " How I pitied the brave Kunzman. He

" must certainly have fought valiantly in
" defence of the count, for he was wound-
" ed and covered with blood. And then
" how affecting was his grief! He wept
" over the dead body, and tore his hair
" with sorrow. I could never have be-
" lieved he had such love for him."

" At these words, Herman shut the
window, and fell almost senseless on the
floor of his prison. " Behold then," cried
he, " how guilt triumphs, and innocence is
" oppressed! Eternal judge! where is thy
" vengeance?"

Presently the rumbling noise of a carriage, and the cries he heard, among which
he thought he could distinguish the plaintive voice of the countess, informed him
that the corpse of the unfortunate count
Cyly was arrived. A cold sweat pervaded
his body; he moved, trembling, towards
the window, but retired before he had
reached it, unable to bear the melancholy
spectacle.

H 3

It is difficult to divine, what were the thoughts and feelings of Herman, during the mournful silence that succeeded this fearful tumult.   A noise at the door of his prison, at length roused him from his gloomy reverie.   The bolts gave way.   A female voice said to him : " Sir Herman, " you are at liberty ?"

" At liberty ! By whose order?"

" By the assistance of a poor girl, who " has taken pity on you, and who wishes, " by a good action, to make some atone- " ment for the many sins she has com- " mitted.   Fly ! fly ! before it be too late !

" Fly ! Innocence never flies !"

" What will your innocence avail you " here ?"

" I will first avenge the blood of count " Peter, by publishing the name of his " cruel assassin.

" But who will listen to you?"

" Sigismond shall listen to me.   I will " unmask to him the hypocrite Barbe."

" My mistress! Oh, I beseech you, do
" not seek your ruin!"

" Barbe, thy mistress? Art thou then
" one of her accomplices?

" I am .... I am .... But for hea-
" ven's sake fly. The countess now rules
" alone in this castle. The king quitted
" it in haste an hour ago. A courier
" brought him news from Prague. Some
" extraordinary revolution is talked of.—
" But what am I doing! Away: lose not
" those precious moments which can never
" be recalled. I must instantly shut the
" tower, where it has been resolved to let
" you perish with hunger. Your escape
" will not be immediately discovered, but
" my absence will be remarked, and you
" will have to reproach yourself with the
" death of her who has sought your deli-
" verance."

Herman no longer objected to follow
her advice. He took the hand of his con-
ductress, and expressed a wish to know the
name of the person who had acquired so

H 4

deep a claim on his gratitude. She complied
with his request, and before they parted, informed him beside, that Kunzman, notwithstanding his wound, and the countess's
intreaties, had been obliged to accompany
the king, who, probably from a remainder
of suspicion, no longer treated him with
his wonted partiality.

CHAPTER XIII.

HERMAN fled, and fled with caution, because he knew that the vengeance of a cruel woman, whose pride he had offended, pursued him. During his journey, which was long, he heard of various events. The emperor Winceslaus was all but deposed: his wife, the incomparable Sophia, courageously shared his troubles. She seemed to have begun to love him just as he became unfortunate. She consoled him; she considered his not having filled the place of Susanna with a new mistress as a merit in him; she was even generous enough to lament the melancholy fate of a woman who had occasioned her so much sorrow. This worthless creature, desirous of forming her taste upon the model of her lover, and of assuming the direction of his orgies, had found it necessary to drink as freely as himself; but her constitution being too feeble to support it, she died in conse-

H 5

quence of her intemperance, without being
in the least regretted by him, to whom she
had sacrificed her health and life. " Wo-
" men," said the emperor, speaking of her
after her death, " are absolutely good for
" nothing, not even for drinking."

While Winceslaus, shut up in a castle,
owed his safety solely to the prudence of
Sophia, whose tender care he repaid after
his manner, the affairs of Sigismond in Hungary had taken a favourable turn; his enemies were humbled, and, by the assistance
of count Cyly, brother to Peter the Weak,
he had re-ascended the throne. He mar-
ried the widow of the deceased count, and
found in this union the deserved chastise-
ment of his perfidy respecting queen Mary,
the princess Helen, and a thousand others.
Barbe ruled him despotically. The only
point she could not obtain from Sigismond
was to keep Hertingshausen in his service.
The remembrance of the kiss, which he
could not help charging on him rather than
on Herman, never escaped from his mind.

Kunzman was obliged therefore to quit the
court and to enter under no very favourable
circumstances, into the service of the elector of Mentz, where perhaps we shall shortly pursue him.

The projects of Sigismond to obtain the
imperial crown did not prove successful.
A great number of princes aspired to it,
among others Robert count palatine, count
Everard of Wirtemberg, and Frederic
duke of Brunswic; and upon one of these
three it was considered as certain that the
election would fall.

Herman no sooner heard that count
Everard and duke Frederic were among the
competitors at Nuremberg, than his doubts
respecting the place to which he should direct his steps were at an end. He had hitherto been ignorant of Ida's abode; but
he now thought it certain that she must be
with her father and her intended spouse.
He ardently wished to see her; he was desirous also of acquainting duke Frederic
with the conspiracies formed against his

life. But the father, the betrothed lover
of Ida were sounds grating to the ears of
Herman. Poor young man! what a prospect for his heart, whether he considered
her as the daughter or the wife of the future
emperor!

Herman was now in the neighbourhood
of Fritzlar, where a rumour prevailed that
the princes of Germany had rejected the
duke of Brunswic, and that, burning with
resentment, the duke had quitted Nuremberg, to return to his own country, accompanied by his brother-in-law, Rodolph of
Saxony. It is easy to imagine the pleasure
our hero derived from the report. This
dangerous rival must then have quitted his
mistress, and had no prospect of obtaining
the title of emperor, so much desired by
count Everard for his son-in-law, should
he be unable to acquire it for himself.—
New hopes sprung up in the mind of our
knight. He beheld every obstacle sur-
mounted, the moment this redoubtable
duke had departed from the field; forget-

ting how few were his pretensions to aspire to the daughter, as it might prove, of an emperor.

Meanwhile, having heard that duke Frederic was to pass by way of Fritzlar, he resolved to introduce himself to this prince, in order to inform him of the danger to which he was exposed. The moment he ceased to consider him as the destined husband of Ida, he felt himself doubly interested in his behalf. He placed himself therefore, under a tree by the side of the highway. The place was solitary. The people of the canton accustomed to see princes pass, waited not in crowds their coming, to assure themselves they were but men.

Herman waited a considerable time. Fatigued with his journey, he at length fell asleep. In this situation he had continued perhaps some hours when he was waked by a fearful dream. He conceived that duke Frederic was torn to pieces by a lion, and that an attempt was made to clothe him in

the skin of the prince's murderer.—Reco-
vering from the terror into which he was
thrown by this dream, he rose and perceived near him a pale and ghastly figure,
with hair dishevelled, and a naked sabre in
his hand.

Herman started back. " What wouldst
" thou do with my sabre?" Cried he, perceiving it in the hands of the stranger.

" Thy sabre !" said the man, instantly
throwing it into the thickest part of the
wood. " Look on the ground ; there lies
" thy sabre. Its terrible appearance
" struck me so forcibly, that I was unable
" to pursue my way ; and suspecting thee
" for an assassin, I drew my own, in order
" to defend myself, if thou shouldst
" awake."

Herman looked, and saw near the place
where he had been sleeping, a sabre reek-
ing with blood. " Wretch !" said he, taking the stranger by the throat, what
" means that bloody weapon? . . . . But,

" heavens? . . . . whom do I see? Kunz-
" man of Hertingshausen, the murderer of
" count Peter!"

Struck with horror, Herman let go his
hold, and Kunzman no sooner found himself disengaged than he fled with all speed,
leaving our knight in the most inconceiva-
ble astonishment.

At the same instant a dreadful clamour
was heard in the wood. One lamented the
loss of his good master. Another exclaimed, " it is here the murder must have
" been committed!" while a third cried,
" No, it was not here that he fell: we
" found his body at a distance. The assas-
" sin however cannot be far; we had once
" almost taken him, but he escaped, and
" bears in his hand the instrument of his
" crime*."

---

* History says, " that duke Frederic entered the wood
alone, leaving his attendants at the distance of a bow-shot.
Kurd, the chief of his guards, impatient at his delay, followed him and found him assassinated. He was time
enough to fee the murderers escape, and even came up
with one of them, whose name was Hertingshausen.

Herman was yet standing with his arms folded, before the sabre of Kunzman, when these frightful sounds assailed his ears, and he now stepped forward to ascertain whether they were real, or a continuance only of the illusions of his dream; but scarcely had he advanced a single step, when twenty voices cried out at once, " There he is! " behold, behold the assassin!" and twenty sabres glittered in his eyes, ready to be drenched in his blood.

Some evil genius seemed to have arranged matters for the very purpose of throwing suspicion on the innocent and favouring the guilty: for who would suppose they beheld a murderer in a person, who, instead of flying, approached with an a.r of tranquillity, which a villain, after the commission of a crime, is incapable of assuming; in a young man whose every feature spoke innocence and candour? The only resemblance between him and Kunzman, the author of the murder, consisted in their armour, and the rose coloured sleeve worn by each, both of them belonging to the same order of knighthood.

Herman had been little accustomed to yield to an enemy without defending himself. He accordingly snatched up the sabre of Kunzman, having no resource but to use the bloody and murderous weapon of that assassin, his own sabre having been taken from him while he had slept, and thrown by Kunzman into the wood.

In those days it was by no means uncommon for a man so far to carry his bravery as to prefer dying in combat, to begging favour of an enemy; as the custom of surrendering voluntarily, in consequence of having discovered a superiority of number, or of strength, was yet not established. Herman laid about him like a true and valorous knight. Two of his opponents were already dead at his feet, and others so severely wounded as to be incapable of resistance; when at length the whole troop rushed on him in a body, threw him to the ground, and would infallibly have deprived him of life, had not their chief interfered, and forbidden them to kill him.

" Stop !' cried Kurd, commander of the guards of the unfortunate duke : " The " villain deserves not to die by the hands of " brave men like you."

" Ah" said one of them, who had ran his sword through the body of Herman after he had been beaten to the ground : " Your interference is too late. I have " given him his dose. See how his life " escapes with his blood! Sweet sacrifice of " vengeance to the departed manes of " Frederic!"

" What hast thou done?" replied Kurd : " Haste instantly to bind up his wound.— " He is not the only criminal; the rest " have fled ; and he must not die till he " has discovered his infamous accom- " plices."

Herman was lying senseless on the ground. His wound being bound up, he was conveyed to an inn in a neighbouring village, whither Rodolph of Saxony, incon-

solable for the loss of his friend, had promised to repair.

"Rodolph shall be thy judge," cried
Kurd, perceiving as they went that Herman began to recover a little from his
swoon : " Thy soul shall not take its flight
" to hell, till we have learned from thy
" mouth the names of thy companions in
" iniquity, that we may have ample ven-
" geance."

Herman made no answer. Probably
he heard not the cruel words that were addressed to him. His head fell on one
shoulder, while his features were expressive
of the acutest anguish; and presently, as
they placed him on the straw at the inn, his
senses a second time forsook him.

Meanwhile enquiries were made respecting duke Rodolph. No person in the village
having heard of him, Kurd dispatched half
his comrades in search of him, remaining
himself with the rest to take care of the
wounded prisoner, and endeavour to pre-

serve the feeble spark of life that seemed every moment about to be extinguished.

Towards evening, however, the senses of Herman returned, and he asked for drink. Wine was given him, and he was presently thought sufficiently strong to answer any questions that might be put to him.

" It is possible," said Kurd, to his fellow guards, " that he may die before the " duke of Saxony arrives, who has per- " haps taken another road. I will inter- " rogate him, therefore, myself, and you " shall be witnesses of his deposition."

" An assassin! the murderer of duke " Frederic! I!" replied Herman, but with a feeble voice, to the first question that was put to him. " O God, the protector " of innocence . . . . !'

" Wilt thou add falsehood to thy crime? " Does not this sabre testify against thee?"

" It was smeared with gore," cried all the witnesses at once, " when we saw thee " take it from the ground to employ it

" against us: the blood of our good master,
" which it had shed, has been mingled with
" ours!"

" Let us be just," said Kurd : " This
" circumstance alone is not sufficient to
" convict him : the sword of an innocent
" person may be made bloody by acci-
" dent. There are things which plead
" more strongly against him. I will even
" suppose that I might be mistaken as to
" his figure and his dress, though I observed
" them too well when I first came up with
" him, and tore off the cloak in which he
" had wrapped himself. But look at the
" sabre; it is that of duke Frederic ; and
" the murderers seized his own sword to
" bathe it in his blood."

The witnesses drew near: having examined it, they kissed the homicide fteel,
exclaiming, " It is indeed the sabre of our
" good duke, as sure as there is a God who
" reigns in Heaven! Let us take vengeance,
" instant vengeance, on his murderer!"

As the light of a lamp, whose wick, almost consumed, when replenished with oil suddenly revives, throws out for an instant a more brilliant splendor, and then is entirely extinguished, such was the effect produced on Herman by the wine he had swallowed. This drink, in his present situation, was actual poison; but for the moment it revived him, and gave him a degree of strength and vivacity almost equal to a person in health. Perhaps, too, his desperate situation, of which he now first became sensible, made so lively an impression on him, that he exerted all his powers, resolving not to die accused of murder without having justified himself.

Herman raised himself, therefore, on his feet, and the inn-keeper with some of his people came to support him.

"No," said he, with firmness, "I am "not the assassin of duke Frederic. The "sabre in question had never been in my "hands till you saw me take it up to defend "myself. . Long . . . . And you must

" surely have perceived me . . . Long had
" I contemplated it with horror, without
" daring to touch it; for I had a presenti-
" ment that it was stained with innocent
" blood . . . ."

" Wretch!' said Kurd, " and hast
" thou then the effrontery to aver this?
" hast thou the effrontery . . . ."

It is unnecessary to relate to the reader
word for word the conversation that passed.
Suffice it to say that the accents of truth
issuing from the mouth of the almost ex-
piring youth, produced at least the effect of
exciting doubts, in the minds of the guards,
of what they had hitherto considered as certain. He related at length all that happened to him in the course of the day; and
both the judges and the spectators found so
much probability in what he said, that they
looked at one another with astonishment,
and were at a loss how to act.

Kurd now recollected a circumstance,
which, in the first impulse of his rage, he
had forgotten; a circumstance that could

not fail either to justify or convict the accused. We have observed that he had once
nearly apprehended the assassin : he had
torn off his cloak, which he seized with one
hand, while with the other he grasped so
strongly the hair of the murderer that he
could not escape without leaving a handful
of it with his adversary. This hair Kurd
had taken care to preserve, and he drew it
from his pocket, in order at once to confound his prisoner, to whom he no longer
knew what to say.   But how great was his
surprise when, looking at this hair, which
was black, he compared it with the light
ringlets that shadowed the pale face of Herman!—" And am I indeed," cried he,
" mistaken? is it possible this man can be
" innocent?"

The inn-keeper, who had hitherto supported Herman on his feet, now let him
sink gently on the straw, and thus interposed, " I would lay my life," said he, that the
" person you have apprehended is not the
" criminal.   It appears to me . . . . . Come

" here, my lads, and look . . . . it appears
" to me that he is the young knight who
" has lodged with us for three or four days
" past."

The servants of the inn-keeper approached. " It is!" cried they at once ;
" It is the good sir Herman of Unna. In-
" deed, sir, he is not, he cannot be an
" assassin."

Herman had in reality staid several
days in this village, where he had given a
thousand proofs of the goodness of his heart.
In every place in which he sojourned he had
made himself friends. It is not therefore to
be wondered at, that, in consequence of the
dispute which now arose between the guards
and the people of the inn, and of the report, spread through the village, that the
young knight had been wounded by the attendants of duke Frederic ; it is not, I say,
to be wondered at, that the inhabitants
flocked together to see him and avenge his
cause. On this occasion the women acted
the most conspicuous part. They abused

and mal-treated the guards, and actually took possession of the unfortunate Herman, who had suffered extremely from the exertions he had made to justify himself, and from the little care that had been taken of him during the uproar excited on his account.

Kurd being at length softened, endeavoured to re-establish peace. " All you " have urged," said he, " is still insuffici- " ent to prove the innocence of this young " man. If he be indeed not guilty, I ar- " dently wish to make reparation for what " he has suffered. But, as you yourselves " know, he may be sir Herman of Unna, " your benefactor, and yet the murderer " of the duke. This handful of hair proves " more than all your vociferation; but even " this is not enough to save him. There " were more persons than one, and though " not the assassin, he may be an accom- " plice. The affair must be carried before " a tribunal more capable of judging; and " if his innocence be there acknowledged,

" we shall be satisfied. For the present I
" leave him to your care. Two of my
" men shall stay to guard him ; and if you
" permit him to escape you must take the
" consequence. So imprudent a step, while
" it would be of no service to him, would
" be certain ruin to yourselves."

A horseman now arrived, bringing information that Rodolph was made prisoner,
and that his people were assembled within
three miles of Fitzlar to fly to his assitance.
The brave Kurd quitted the inn without
losing a moment. As faithfully attached to
Rodolph as to the unfortunate Frederic, he
would on no account have been absent from
so important an expedition.

CHAPTER XIV.

HERMAN remained in the care of his former host.   Though his wounds were nót mortal, the great quantity of blood he had lost, the efforts he had made, and the wine he had drank, rendered them dangerous.—— He was for several days between life and death, and would infallibly have perished but for the humanity of the honest pea-sants.   An old shepherd, the oracle of the village, was his surgeon, and cured him by, an ointment composed of various simples, among which our manuscript mentions, as the principal, mpss taken from a dead man's skull and blanched by the rays of the sun : a fact which we pretend not to dispute, hav-ing little skill in such matters.*

* The moss which grows on the skull of a man un-buried, was celebrated, in the days of superstition, for its medicinal virtues, and made a grand ingredient of the famous fympathetic powder, which was faid to cure the

By degrees our hero recovered so as to be able to walk. He conversed freely with his hosts on the terrible adventure that had so nearly cost him his life, on the gratitude he owed them, and the recompense that was due to their generosity: but he had neither speech nor ears when they advised him secretly to make his escape. In vain was it represented to him, that he might find it difficult to clear himself before prejudiced judges; in vain was he told that there was nobody to detain him, the men left to guard him having withdrawn: he remained true to the principle he had lately avowed at the castle of Cyly, *innocence never flies*, and resolved to wait for his accusers; or, if they did not come, to repair to Nuremberg, and take for his judges the princes who were there assembled.

The latter was the measure he adopted. The people of duke Rodolph, among whom

most desperate wound, at the distance of half the globe, merely by being applied to the weapon with which the wound was inflicted. T.

I 3

was now the faithful Kurd, more attentive
to the means of delivering their master,
than of avenging duke Frederic, appeared
to have wholly forgotten him. He was
forced, therefore, to proceed to Nuremberg,
and deliver himself up to the princes of the
German empire, in whose justice he had the
fullest confidence; or submit to bear the
disgrace of being suspected of murder. His
arguments at length brought over his hosts
to his opinion, and they accompanied him
on his way to a distance from the village,
not leaving him till they arrived at the fatal
tree, where treacherous sleep had been so
near delivering him into the arms of death.

" Let this tree, said he, as he quitted the
crowd that accompanied him, " Let this
" tree testify my innocence! You, my
" friends, believe it only from attach-
" ment to me: but why cannot this
" trunk speak, this trunk, under the
" branches of which I so peaceably slept,
" when the lion that had devoured duke
" Frederic presented itself before me in my

" dream, and attempted to cover me with
" his blood? Why are not these leaves so
" many tongues to attest the truth? Why
" do not those aerial spirits, that invisibly
" hovered over Kunzman and me, appear,
" and bear witness against the murderer?"

" Give me leave, sir knight," said one
of the oldest of the company, " to give you
" a word of advice. You know what we
" think of you; but the princes into whose
" hands you are going to place yourself, are
" not all Roberts count palatine, or Alberts
" of Austria. There are amongst them
" many, whose penetration is not clear
" enough to discover innocence enveloped
" in such obscurity; and perhaps there may
" be others, who would not be sorry to see
" the innocent suspected of their own hor-
" rid crime. Above all, trust not to the
" elector of Mentz. Since the assassination
" of duke Frederic, strange reports have
" been spread in the neighbourhood; and
" of this at least we are certain, that he and
" the duke were never friends."

I 4

Having received this advice, Herman pursued his way to Nuremberg; where, on his arrival, his first business was to inquire after Ida: a circumstance from which the reader may possibly infer, that the hope of seeing her was as great an inducement to him to visit that city, as the desire of justifying his innocence.

He soon learnt that the count of Wirtemberg had just departed on a short journey, and that in the mean time his daughter remained alone at his house, out of which, however, she was never seen. He longed to have an interview with her; he was aware of the difficulty of the enterprize; but ought he, because success was uncertain, to hazard the never seeing her more?

Love rendered him bold and ingenious, and the project with which it inspired him was so simple, and so easy of execution, that it appeared impossible for him not to succeed. Who, indeed, would dare shut the door against a knight, professing to be sent to the princess from the count of Wirtemberg, her father? He was introduced, therefore, without delay, and presented himself before her.

" Herman!" exclaimed Ida, the instant he fell at her feet; " Herman sent here by " my father !"

" Would Ida be offended, should love " have dictated to me this innocent strata-" gem ?"

" O Herman! Herman!" resumed the princess, stooping towards him: " where " hast thou been wandering so long? And " whence that deadly paleness? Whence " those languid eyes ?"

We have already more than once had occasion to remark, that our hero was never so well received by his mistress as when he came upon her unexpectedly. Of this she now gave a fresh proof. It was some time before she withdrew herself from his embrace, before she represented to him what decorum required of her; and he was too sensible of his advantage, to recal her from

I 5

her pleasing self-forgetfulness by any ill-
timed question.

"Rise, sir Herman: said Ida at length,.
blushing and turning away her lovely face:
"how strangely are we acting! . . . . You
"said you brought news of my father:
"is he well? will he be soon at home?"

Herman had yet not mentioned the name
count Everard, but he did not think fit to
tell her so: he thought, no doubt, that, either
she knew not what she said, or to hide her
emotion asked the first question that oc-
curred.

On her invitation he sat down by her
side, and, after a short interval, during
which, neither well knew what to say, a
kind of conversation between them began,
which became imperceptibly more regular,
and they reciprocally informed each other
of what it was of most importance for them
to know.

Ida's tale was not long. Her life, under
the direction of a rigid father, was as uniform as that of other young ladies of her

time. In those rude and unpolished days, young women were seldom permitted to show themselves in public, and their conduct was scrupulously watched, that nothing might occur to tarnish their reputation.—— Though the daughters of princes were sometimes an exception to this rule, count Everard was resolved, respecting Ida, to pursue the established custom. He had always present to his imaginasion that Herman of Unna, who had leaped from the balcony of his daughter's apartment into the garden to escape being seen, and who had so powerful an advocate in the empress.—— Besides, Ida was far too handsome to be exposed to the eyes of all the libertine youths whom the diet had attracted to Nuremberg. The late duke of Brunswic himself had seen her but twice, tho' the count had cast his eyes upon him for a son-in-law; but the duke was to become the spouse of Ida only on condition of his obtaining the imperial crown.

Herman was delighted with the princess's recital, which she delivered with her
wonted frankness. In his heart, he thanked
count Everard for having so carefully
watched over his treasure, and he openly
applauded himself, on the cunning with
which he had cheated the vigilance of her
guards. She hinted to him, not to be too
much elated, as he was indebted for his
success solely to chance, and the absence
of a strict duenna, who was gone to church,
and whose return she expected every moment.

The most important subject of conversation, had not yet been touched by our
two lovers, and there was no time to lose.
Herman, therefore, hastened to relate his
adventures, and the motives of his arrival
at Nuremberg.

It would be superfluous to mention, the
deep impression made on the heart of the
young princess by his tale. Of all the
dangers her dear Herman had run, that to
which he was at present exposed, appeared

to her the most terrible. She trembled to think that he was going voluntarily to present himself before judges, whom she was far from knowing well enough to be certain, that they would effectually protect him.—— She prayed, she intreated him, with tears in her eyes, to wait for his accusers, adding, that he ought to consider himself as fully justified, if they did not appear; God, and his own conscience, completely acquitting him. At any rate, prudence required him to provide for his safety by flight, till the particulars of the engagement, which had been reported to have taken place between the ravishers of, duke Rodolph and his people were known, as perhaps, it would then be found, that not one of his accusers remained alive to testify against him.

Her looks were expressive of the mingled sentiments of love and fear, as she thus endeavoured to convince him, by reasons of every kind, good as well as bad, of the necessity of his absconding: but his resolution was unshaken.

" Should I be worthy of thee," cried
he, " could I for a moment deserve thy
" hand, thou model of perfection, if I
" sought not to clear myself from the charge
" of murder? . . . . No: it suffices not that
" God and my own conscience, that you
" and other virtuous minds are assured of
" my innocence; the whole world ought to
" know, that Herman of Unna is not an
" assassin; that at least it is not on such an
" account, he is forbidden to aspire to the
" hand of the princess of Wirtemberg."

CHAPTER XV.

THE lovers now separated. Herman quitted the princess, with a determination to proceed in the execution of his design; and Ida remained plunged in the profoundest sorrow. The remembrance, however, of a similar danger, to which she had herself been exposed, and the surprising manner in which she had been extricated from it, prevented her fears from being converted into despair.—" The " tribunal before which I was cited, was it " not infinitely more formidable?" said she to herself. " This at least will be " held in open day, and in the face of the " world; whereas mine was covered with " eternal night . . . . Yet I escaped . . . . " Be not discouraged, Ida; he is innocent; " he appears voluntarily, without being " accused; and, should every other means " of defence be wanting, still he has his " sword. No: do not despair. The or- " deal to which he submits himself, will re- " down to his glory, and perhaps contri- " bute to his happiness and thy own!"

Herman had quitted the apartment but a few minutes, when the Duenna returned, who seldom left her, except when, to procure a few hours relief from her company, Ida feigned indisposition. The princess had been a stranger to falsehood and dissimulation, till a strict and suspicious watch over her, had in a manner compelled her to have recourse to them. She trembled lest the name of the young man who had visited her should be asked. He had entered and gone out in presence of all the people who waited in the anti-chamber. She was too noble-minded to desire her domestic to conceal the circumstance; and she expected every moment, that Cunegunda would put some question to her, which she should not know how to answer. For this time, however, her alarms were false; even her melancholy did not appear to be observed; nor was it till the evening of the following day, that the old lady introduced a conversation, little calculated to give consolation to our fair mourner.

" Will your tears never cease, prin-
" cess?" said the duenna; " It appears to
" me, that they flow more copiously within
" this day or two."

" It may be so."

" And for what reason? .... Why
" conceal it from me? Is it a crime for a
" young lady of your age to be in love; or,
" when so unfortunate in her attachment,
" to lament the loss of her lover?"

The tears of Ida increased.

" Poor child! To lose him in so terrible
" a manner too, by murder! .... Yet you
" have one comfort left; the crime will be
" revenged; his death will not go unpunish-
" ed; the criminal has surrendered himself."

Ida dried her tears, and looking sted-
fastly at the duenna, with a countenance
of despair: " Of whom," said she, " art
" thou talking?"

" The assassin of duke Frederic, your
" betrothed husband, I say, has surrendered
" himself into the hands of justice."

" Well! And he has been acquitted, I
" hope? You know..... I know.....
" No matter, he is known to be innocent."

" Permit me, princess, to ask, in my
" turn, of whom you are talking?"

" Of sir .... Oh! my head is bewil-
" dered! I know not what I say. Pray, if
" you must talk, talk by yourself, for you see
" I am not in a state to answer you."

The old lady began a tale, which made
so deep an impression upon Ida, that at its
conclusion her senses forsook her. How
was it possible for her to hear without emotion, that Herman had appeared before the
tribunal of princes; that he had faithfully
related every circumstance both for and
against himself; and that, instead of being
instantly acquitted, he had been sent to prison, and ordered to be closely confined, till
farther information could be obtained.

" I entréat you," said Ida, after she had
come to herself, and been tormented with a
thousand questions respecting her sudden
indisposition, which she answered, no

doubt, incoherently enough. " I entreat
" you to begin your tale again. If the de-
" sire of seeing duke Frederic avenged, be,
" as you suppose, the cause of my illness,
" you ought to conceal nothing from me.
" Tell me then, in the first place, who were
" his . . . . . who were the judges of the
" stranger?"

" Judges, indeed! God and all his
" saints forgive them!" cried the duenna:
" Such judges were surely never seen since
" the world began! I except, however, the
" elector of Mentz; he did his duty; it was
" he who ordered the murderer to be seized
" and sent to prison."

" Seized and sent to prison! Were you
" present?"

" Yes: the judges were sitting in open
" court as I came this morning from mass."

" It is impossible! The world cannot
" be so blind, as not to see his innocence
" . . . . But tell me, who were the rest of
" his judges ?"

" The majority were favourable to him,
" and would have acquitted him, but they
" were over-ruled."

" Worthy, virtuous men! . . . . . But
" their names, their names, Cunegunda !"

" You know, as well as I, the prince
" who has the most influence here, and
" who is sure to take care, that no good
" shall be done. You must not, there-
" fore, expect to be the daughter of an em-
" peror, as long as . . . ."

" Oh! do not thus urge my patience
" beyond bearing! Let who will be em-
" peror, so this poor . . . ."

" Ah! princess, princess! interrupted
Cunegunda, holding up her finger in an
action of threatening . . . . " But, no
" matter; I will indulge you for once.—
" The persons most inclined to favour this
" man, for whom, God knows why, you
" are so greatly interested, were Robert
" count Palatine, duke Albert, and old
" Jadoc of Moravia; all rivals, and secret

" enemies of your father; perhaps, too,
" accomplices in the death of your pro-
" mised husband, and therefore, defenders
" of the assassin, who certainly would not
" have presented himself, had he not been
" sure of finding in them an unjust pro-
" tection."

" And the elector of Mentz?" said Ida.

" He alone did his duty. He ordered
" the murderer to be detained, in spite of
" the opposition of his partisans, the num-
" ber of whom increased every moment,
" and who would forthwith have set him
" at liberty."

" And do you think, my dear Cune-
" gunda, he runs no risk of being assassi-
" nated in his prison?"

" What the murderer?".

" Oh, do not give him so odious an ap-
" pellation! How can you be so imbittered
" against a stranger?"

" A stranger! In truth, princes, I be-
" lieve the chevalier Unna is more a

" stranger to me than to you : but I
wish your father was returned."

From this period there subsisted a cool-
ness between the princess and her governante. Ida, ashamed of having suffered
her secret to be thus penetrated, hated the
enemy of the innocent Herman ; while the
old duenna, having learnt all she wanted
to know, and having no need of any fresh
explanation, took care to be silent respecting the farther proceedings in this affair.
Indeed she had nothing to communicate
but what would have been pleasing to the
empress, and her heart was too black, too
malevolent, to think of affording consolation, however oppreffed might be the mind
that wanted it.

Herman had presented himself before
the princes. His simple and ingenuous
tale, clothed in the artless language of
truth; his interesting figure; his open
countenance, no equivocal index of the
candour and goodness of his heart; his vo-
luntary appearance; all spoke in his favour,

and would have been sufficient to exculpate
him from the crime of which he was accused, had even no other witnesses appeared to attest his innocence. But the
peasants of the village where Herman had
been cured of his wounds, having his safety
at heart, had followed him, and presented
themselves in court the moment he appeared before his judges.

In those days justice was administered
in a more expeditious and summary way
than at present. The friends of Herman, who
were at the same time the friends of virtue,
Robert, Albert and Jadoc; had too ardent a
desire of rendering innocence triumphant,
and of humbling the elector of Mentz, not
to insist on the trial's being resumed the
next day; and it was then that our hero was
completely acquitted and obtained his discharge. Kurd, commander of the guards
of the murdered prince, appeared, and was
examined apart. His deposition agreed
perfectly with that of Herman, and he declared, that he had no complaint to make

against him, but, on the contrary, that he believed him innocent. He produced the lock of hair which he had torn from the head of the assassin as he escaped, and which evidently belonged not to the prisoner.

The friends of our knight listened with great pleasure to this deposition; but the elector of Mentz did not appear to be satisfied till he learnt that Kunzman had ultimately escaped, as well as an accomplice that was with him. The enemies of Herman were then desirous of inferring that he might be the accomplice who fled. But Jadoc observed, that it was for them, not the prisoner, to prove this; which, from the testimonies exhibited of his innocence, he was sure they would find impossible.

To relate all that was urged on both sides the question would be tedious: suffice it therefore to say, that Herman's innocence was judicially acknowledged, and that many of the princes could not avoid

entertaining suspicions of John of Mentz,
to whom they scrupled not to hint them.—
It may be proper also to add, that Kunzman, the murderer of duke Frederic, was
in the service of the elector.

Of the several princes, whose affection
our hero had gained on this occasion, not
one was more attached to him than the
young Albert of Austria, whose character
was regarded as a miniature likeness of Herman. History speaks highly of the virtues
of Albert, and particularly of his generosity. Judge, reader, from this, what must
have been the character of the chevalier·
Unna.

The young knight had the good fortune
to please duke Albert at first sight. His
great qualities, far from exciting envy in
this prince, determined him to unite himself to our youth by the bonds of the ten-
derest friendship, and to set aside all difference of rank and birth.

The trial being at an end, duke Albert
gave Herman an invitation to come and see

him. It was with difficulty he could refrain from testifying at once the inclination he felt for him ; but prudence required
that he should avoid, by a too sudden dis-
closure, exciting pride in him, and jealousy
perhaps in others. Herman was requested
to relate his adventures; a request with
which he complied, and he spoke with so
much frankness of what concerned himself,
and so much discretion of those who figured
in his story, that the good opinion Albert
had conceived of him was so far increased
as to make him forget his resolution; and
Herman, ere he quitted the house, where a
few hours before his fate was pending, was
received into the number of the principal gentlemen of that prince, justly
esteemed one of the most virtuous of his
time.

Ida knew nothing of this happy change.
Her governante, as we have observed, did
not think proper to acquaint her with any
thing pleasing respecting her lover, of

whom count Everard, when he gave his daughter to her charge, had particularly directed her to be cautious, but who, notwithstanding, as the duenna learnt, had been adroit enough to elude her vigilance, and procure an interview with the princess.

The sole thing of which Ida was informed was, that Herman's fate was that day to be decided. It is not to be wondered at, therefore, that she passed the night which preceded it without sleep, and the morning in extreme agitation.

From her window she had seen the princes assembled at the house of old Jadoc. She felt, as she saw those enter whom Cunegunda had mentioned as friendly to Herman, a sentiment of gratitude, and of hatred at sight of the others, particularly the elector of Mentz. The prisoner was brought under a strong guard. By their armour she could distinguish the people of the late duke of Brunswic. The duenna

K 2

explained to her their intentions with the most provoking malignity. The trial had lasted for some hours, yet nothing could induce her to quit the window but her extreme weariness, which at length she could no longer support.

The princess had been put to bed, and Cunegunda, who believed her to be asleep, had gone out in quest of news to satisfy her malicious curiosity. She soon learned, what would have imparted instant ease and revived the drooping spirits of her charge, but she was too cruel to administer the remedy.

Meanwhile Ida had lain on her bed without sleeping. An uncommon noise, which she heard in the street, excited her attention; she forgot her feebleness, and ran to the window. The people were rushing in crowds from the house of Jadoc, and she fancied that she could distinguish in their shouts some words of comfort.

The crowd increased. Presently duke Albert appeared on horseback with his attendants. The person nearest to him, and who seemed rather to ride by his side than to follow him, was a young man of the size and ftature of Herman, and accoutred like him. The duke was in familiar conversation with him, and appeared to pay him particular attention.

Ida opened the window to obtain a better view. The cavalcade now paffed near her. The young man, whose rose-coloured sleeve she could eafily distinguish, was no other than Herman himself. She felt as if she should expire with joy. The moment our knight of fidelity perceived her, he kissed the badge of his order, as if to say: " for thee only do I wear it." Duke Albert also saw and respectfully faluted the princess. A confused murmur was heard among the people, which presently broke out into shouts of " long live duke Albert, " the protector of innocence! long live the " good sir Herman, so honourably ac- " quitted!"

K 3

The rapture of Ida was so great that she could no longer support it. She turned round, and flew with open arms to Cunegunda, who at that moment entered. " He is saved!" cried she; " he is saved!" and instantly fainted.

CHAPTER XVI.

DAYS and weeks passed away. Ida thought herself happy in knowing that her beloved chevalier was secure under the protection of duke Albert, and in seeing him pass every day beneath her window. Yet she could not help regretting that she was not permitted to speak to him. She saw him, but she saw him only at a distance; all his endeavours to obtain access to her being frustrated by the vigilance of Cunegunda. Sweet mixture of pleasure and pain which, connoisseurs tell us, enhances the enjoyments of love.

Meanwhile Ida continually hoped to see her lover still nearer, and beyond this she had scarcely a desire. It was possible, she thought, that, by some lucky chance, he might again deceive the Argus' eyes of the duenna; or that they might meet at church, or at some place of entertainment, which Ida now seemed extremely desirous of fre-

K 4

quenting. But Cunegunda was inexorable.
She could not conceive how so virtuous a
princess should imbibe all at once a taste
for balls and other amusements, where
young libertines of fashion were sure to
assemble, or at least she pretended not to
be able to conceive it; and consoled her
with the hope of the speedy return of her
father.

At length the count of Wirtemberg arrived. He had a long conference with the
governante, of which his cold and reserved
behaviour to Ida was not the only consequence; for whenever he returned from
the assembly of the princes, whether they
had met on business or on pleasure, he appeared extremely out of humour, and frequently treated her with harshness and as-
perity.

One day Ida happened to be at the window with her father, when Herman and
duke Albert passed by. As his mistress was
not alone, the knight kissed not his rose-
coloured sleeve, but he made her a re-

spectful obeisance. Ida blushed, and was silent. But presently, reflecting that her silence might appear like affectation, and that it would be more natural to make some remark on what was then the universal topic of conversation, she said, with some hesitation: " Sir Herman of Unna is.... " is much to be pitied .... is deserving " of the highest commendation .... his " situation was extremely perilous .... How " happy .. that ... he is so warmly esteem- " ed by duke Albert .... and .... that his " innocence has been acknowledged."

Count Everard pretended not to remark the confusion of his daughter. He answered only, in a tone of peevishness, to the latter part of her speech: that duke Albert was fond of every man that at all resembled him, and that with respect to Herman's innocence, new charges were continually rising up against him, which rendered it extremely dubious.—Ida requested an explanation, but the count left her without giving her an answer.

K 5

She now exerted herself for some days, so far to master her feelings, as to be able to speak of Herman without emotion; an attempt in which she at length succeeded.—— This was a necessary step, as she had enquiries to make, which, without the practice of a little address, she could not have satisfied.

" Sir Herman, I find, is not so innocent " as he appeared to be," said she to Cunegunda one day, when, after their return from mass, the chevalier had bowed to her as he passed.

" I told you so at first," replied the duenna.

" But what new proofs have they al- " ledged against him ?"

" Oh, enough, princess, proof enough ! " Has not a sabre, with his name engraved " on it, been found in the forest, a very " little way from the spot where the duke " of Brunswic was assassinated. And did " not Kunzman of Hertingshausen, who " has since been apprehended, and who, a

" few days ago, received the reward of his
" crime, declare, before he died, that Her-
" man was his accomplice?"

Ida turned pale, fixed her eyes on the
duenna, and was unable to speak.

" Beside, was not Herman in the ser-
" vice of king Sigismond, who, at the insti-
" gation of his wicked wife, hated, it seems,
" duke Frederic, and sought to take his
" life."

The princess recollected, that Herman
had mentioned this circumstance in the account he had given her of his history. She
trembled, her paleness increased. She recollected also, that one of the motives which
had induced her lover to repair to Nuremberg, was to acquaint duke Frederic with
the conspiracy forming against him.

" But what tends most to throw suspi-
" cion on him," continued Cunegunda, " is
" the advantage he would have reaped
" from the death of the duke or rather
" which he foolishly promised himself he
" should reap."

" Advantage! what advantage?" Cried
Ida with trepidation, seizing the hand of
Cunegunda.

" Sweet simplicity! said the governante.
" And you really cannot guess? You do not
" know that the duke of Brunswic was
" betrothed to the princess of Wirtemberg,
" and that Sir Herman of Unna is her
" lover?"

Cunegunda, as she uttered these words,
which were accompanied with a malicious
smile, withdrew, and left Ida in a state difficult to describe. It will not be supposed
that the venom which fell from the lips of
this fury, was capable of infecting the mind of
the princess with doubts respecting the young
knight's innocence; but this much is certain,
that from the manner in which the accusation had been stated to her, she feared it
might be made to assume a face very unfavourable to her lover, and that thus he would
be plunged into fresh misfortunes.

What indeed could be more alarming?
Meanwhile there was one thing, and but one

that tended to quiet her apprehensions: she had heard that a person once declared innocent, could not be tried again on the same charge. The calm produced by this reflection was however, of short duration. A considerable intimacy took place between her father and John of Mentz. She trembled whenever she saw this enemy of her lover enter the house. At length his visits became so frequent, that suspicion crept into her mind, and she sought to discover their motive.

The delicate Ida, while the daughter of a simple citizen, had never so far degraded herself as to act the mean part of a listener. Whether she had acquired this new talent from her acquaintance with courts, or whether love had endowed her with it, or whether it were the mere effects of chance that she had fallen asleep behind the hangings in her father's closet, one day when the duke of Mentz had a private conference with him, we pretend not to decide: the reader may solve the enigma as he thinks

best. · She overheard however a conversation in which the name of Herman was frequently repeated; and from the following
letter we may *guess* what was its nature, what
she thought of it, and how she determined
to act.   We say, guess, because, the mystery
having never been fully explained, we have
only our penetration to guide us.

LETTER *from* IDA *of* WIRTEMBERG, *to*
HERMAN *of* UNNA.

HERMAN, is it a dream? Or is it a
reality? I have learnt things that most nearly concern you.   Consider what I am going
to tell you at least as a truth.   Obey my
injunctions: it is your Ida who exacts obe-
dience . . . . Fly, Herman, fly! Vengeance
pursues thee! . . . . Thy prince, exalted as
is his goodness, great as is his power, will
not dare be thy protector.   The INVISIBLES
are thine enemies!

This single sentence, I first thought would
be sufficient to induce you to depart, the

only step that now remains for you, and I
had intended to close with it my letter. I
am obliged to steal from sleep the moments
I devote to you, and, in my present situation, I am unable to write much. But my
fears whisper that you may refuse to obey
me, that you may regard my dream as one
of the ordinary reveries to which no faith is
to be given. I will therefore tell you all,
that you may judge for yourself of the
dangers that threaten you.

I heard two men talking of you. One
of them appeared to be my father. But
no, it could not be he! for can the father
of Ida be the enemy of innocence? Could
he be influenced by the perfidious insinua-
tions of a villain, who wishes perhaps to
escape the punishment of his own crime by
charging it on you? . . . . I listened, secretly listened . . . . in a dream, as it seems to
me, for your Ida is not accustomed to such
practices when awake . . . and I heard these
men say to one another, that you were the
murderer of duke Frederic. Your sabre

found near the place where he had fallen,
the deposition of Kunzman at the scaffold,
and the secret enmity you were supposed to
bear to the betrothed spouse of Ida of Wirtemberg, were the arguments employed to
prove your guilt: it was added, that the
princes having acquitted you would be of no
avail ; your crime was of a nature to come
within the cognizance of another tribunal
. . . . Oh, Herman! That infernal tribunal,
which your Ida too well knows.

My dream is not yet finished. You
know there are dreams which have the
same duration and the same consistency as
the events of our lives which pass when
we are awake . . . . I heard, I thought, the
conversation I have related, word for
word; and I immediately began to reflect
on the means of saving yon. Some days
elapsed. I saw a number of strangers in
my father's house, among whom I once
observed Walter, the man with one hand,
I remember him well. A journey was
talked of, which my father was about to

undertake. I guessed what was its object.
I bribed one of the servants, appointed to
attend him, and with difficulty prevailed
on him to let me take his place. I disguised myself in the black dress which he
brought me, and repaired to my post.—
We set off. The count of Wirtemberg
was attended only by me and another domestic.

Our way was not long. Strange as it
may seem, we entered, I thought, that
ruinous building, which perhaps you have
observed, at a little distance north of the
city . . . . But for heaven's, sake, Herman
be discreet; occasion not our ruin! You
are not ignorant how important it is to
keep silence on this subject. Beside, is it
not all a dream?

The count and his principal domestic
entered without any question being asked.
My figure probably appearing new to the
three persons who guarded the gate, they
examined me by some very extraordinary
questions. They asked me the four ways

to hell, and I answered in the words I had
been taught the same evening by the servant who yielded me his place. They farther asked me, how many steps led to the
judgment seat on which sat the Eternal to
administer justice. I answered thirty; for
I recollected that to be the number I counted, you knew upon what occasion, and
which I had been obliged to ascend with
such feelings of horror. They shook their
heads, blindfolded me, and let me pass.
The number thirty saved my life. I wan-
dered in the dark: I had neither supporter
nor guide. I counted the steps, and having ascended thirty, the way became level.
My eyes were then uncovered.

I found myself in a place similar to what
you have perhaps seen. The signal was
given, and the session commenced. Accusations were read and some witnesses deposed against a prince, whom they charged
with being the murderer of duke Frederic.
Immediately one of the judges rose and
swore that he was innocent. An oath of

this nature, you know, once saved the life of an innocent person! why might it not be equally capable of saving that of a guilty one?

To these accusations, to these witnesses, others succeeded. Your name, Herman, your name was pronounced! But no one would swear for you. I was going to advance, when the man with one hand, whom I then first observed by my side, held me back, threatening me with his finger. In short, you were accused and condemned. "Let vengeance, secret as the night, pur- "sue his steps! Let punishment invisibly "await him!" cried a voice from the throne. "When awake, deceive him by false pre- "tences, and draw him into some snare "that may facilitate the execution of his "sentence. Let the poignard watch the "moment of his sleep. Let him be put to "death wherever he be found alone. Let "his bosom-friend become his executioner; "let him entice him into some solitary "place, and massacre him in open day, in

" the face of that heaven which he has
" offended by the sight of innocent blood.
" Frederic lost his life in secret, and with-
" out any warning : so perish, with all his
" sins upon his head, Herman of Unna !"

As the last words were uttered I should
certainly have screamed with terror, had
not my protector stopped my mouth. It
was he also, I believe, who conveyed me
more dead than alive out of this assembly
of demons. He had discovered me notwithstanding my disguise. He loaded me
with reproaches on my imprudence; and
left me at the gate of my father's house,
after having exacted a promise of silence,
which I have kept as faithfully as was
possible.

What was I now to do? Escape and fly
to you ; or wait the return of my father,
and abide his wrath? Already by the light
of the moon I saw him at a distance accompanied by his domestic. I adopted the
most ready expedient: I knocked at the
door; it was opened ; and I rushed to my

apartment. Cunegunda was astonished at my having so completely deceived her vigilance, and that, while she believed me asleep . . . . But what am I doing? . . . . . Is it not, however, a dream . . . . Yet again I charge you to fly. Fly, Herman, fly! The secret avengers pursue you: they thirst for your blood! . . . . I ought not to warn you of this; but surely I may relate a dream.

CHAPTER XVII.

HERMAN, as we have observed, was sufficiently happy to have found, in his master, a friend. No sooner had he recovered himself from the perturbation in which he was thrown, by the preceding letter, brought to him by a stranger, than he hastened to duke Albert, presented him the fatal scroll. They consulted together, and duke Albert was finally of opinion, that Herman had no other means of saving himself from his pursuers than by flight; and that even this would be futile, unless he could keep himself concealed, or obtain the protection of some superior power.—— "We must part, Herman," said he, "We "must part. Ida is in the right. Thy "prince is too weak to defend thee against "the arms of these invisible avengers."

"What, leave you," replied Herman, "on account of a dream!"

" And can you seriously, my friend,
" believe it to be a dream? No, no: obey
" the princess then, and begone."

" But .... whither can I go?"

" To king Sigismond."

" I, become the slave of the vilest of
" women!" replied Herman, forgetting that
Albert was soon to be related to the royal
house, by marrying Elizabeth, daughter of
Sigismond and Mary.

Albert smiled, and thus continued:—
" Go then to the duke of Saxony, the chief
" of all the secret tribunals. He is best
" able to protect you, if you can prove to
" him, satisfactorily, your innocence."

" But Rodolph, being the friend and
" relation of the unfortunate duke of
" Brunswick, is perhaps already too much
" prejudiced against me, to listen to the
" language of truth."

" What think you, of your relation,
" the old count of Unna? He is one of the
" chiefs of the secret tribunals of Westpha-

" lia, and will surely not refuse you pro-
" tection."

" What! the avowed enemy of our fa-
" mily! . . . . I dare not trust him."

" Have you ever seen him? Do you at
" all know how he is disposed towards
" you?"

" No."

" Herman, I know him.   The count
" of Unna is a man of frankness, sin-
" cerity and truth.   You have never, I
" think, offended him? Go to him then:
" you may rely on his protection."

" His enmity against the house of Unna,
" was occasioned by the contention of the
" knights of St. Martin with count Wir-
" temberg.   I was then but eight years
" old."

" Take my advice, Herman,   throw
" thyself into his arms; he will defend thee,
" and render thy innocence triumphant."

Herman obeyed, and the next night set
off for Westphalia, without having been
able, notwithstanding the many efforts he

made, to thank the princess of Wirtemberg, either personally or by letter. Meanwhile Ida passed her days in sorrow, in the house of her father. Cunegunda watched her more narrowly than ever, and the count of Wirtemberg manifested in his behaviour to her the utmost distrust. The flight of Herman, which was soon known, operated to render her situation still worse. Incessantly tormented with captious questions and oblique reproaches, she lamented her rank, and regretted that she was not still, what she had so long been supposed to be, the daughter of a virtuous citizen. O Munster, how many sighs were drawn from her, by the remembrance of thy peaceful habitation at Prague! How many tears attested her ardent desire to see thee, to ask thy counsel, and to obtain thy assistance, in circumstances so difficult! " Ah!" said she, " he promised Herman never to forsake me, " and yet years are passed away! . . . ."

Ida had forgotten, that, to save her life, Munster had entered into that secret society, which despotically ruled its members, and could, with absolute authority, determine the place where they should reside, and the employments they should undertake. Munster had before obeyed no laws but those of virtue and his own heart. But since his taking this rash step, of entering into a society of the nature of which he was ignorant, the count of Wirtemberg had been his master; and we have had more proofs than one, that the count had much rather he should be at Prague, than near his daughter.

The heart of count Everard, since the occurrence of a late event, of which he, as well as Ida, avoided any mention, seemed alienated from his daughter. His conduct displayed something more than indifference, it appeared to border on hatred. His mind was in a constant state of disquietude, and every instant he was changing his designs. At length he one day declared, all of a sudden, that he was under the necessity of quitting Germany, to seek his safety in some foreign land.

" Your safety!" replied Ida, with astonishment and trembling.

" Yes, traitress! And it is you, or at
" least your imprudence that drives me
" hence. The crimes of children are im-
" puted to their parents."

"´Is it possible," cried Ida, clasping her hands and weeping : " Is it possible, I can
" have such a fault to reproach myself
" with !"

" You have sacrificed your father, to
" save your unworthy lover."

" " Alas! I knew not the consequences of
" what I did, and .... Herman was in-
" nocent !"

" I thought otherwise. His crime was
" represented to me so clearly, that I could
" not doubt. But I can now almost be-
" lieve him innocent, since I am myself
" likely to become the victim of appear-
" ances."

L 2

" What are those appearances, then?
" Oh, tell me!" exclaimed Ida, falling at
his feet.

" Of having taken you to a place, where
" you had no right to appear; of having
" acquainted Herman with the sentence
" that was passed upon him, and assisted
" his escape."

" It is I, it is I alone who am guilty!
" and to save you, I will declare it before
" the whole world."

" It is too late! It is too late!" replied
count Everard, pushing her from him.—
" Farewel! Be happy if thou canst! I must
" leave thee to thy fate."

The count departed, leaving his daughter in the utmost anguish. Grief for the
situation of her lover, and her father, and
the severe reproaches she made herself,
were almost too much for the human frame
to support, and in a few days reduced her
to the brink of the grave. We may doubt
whether the danger to which she was personally exposed, was considered by her as

any augmentation of her sufferings. Self seemed out of the question, seemed to be a thing to which she was totally indifferent, and some strong external impulse was necessary to excite her to think of her security.

One night, when it was late, Cunegunda, the most obliging of creatures, now that Ida was her own mistress, entered, and announced a stranger. The stranger stood at the door, and asked to speak with the princess in private.

" Do you know me? said he, after looking at her for some time.

She hesitated.

" Do you recollect this arm?" added he, throwing back his cloak.

Ida observed the deficiency of the hand, and recognized Walter.

" Can you not guess what brings me
" hither? . . . . Your safety I
" come to warn you . . . . Since the de-
" parture of your father, you are yourself
" in the greatest danger. If you persist in

L 3

" remaining here, the past, as well as the
" present, will be examined anew.   It is
" absolutely necessary that you should fly
" . . . . . O princess! what unhappi-
" ness has your imprudence been the oc-
" casion of! . . . . Where is the pre-
" sumptuous man that dared lend you his
" dress for this adventure? Where is your
" father, who is suspected of having been
" privy to it? And what is to become of
" me, who was totally ignorant of the affair,
" but am now involved in it by my com-
" passion? . . . . You know, that I did
" not discover you, till it was too late; till
" you had actually seen what no profane
" eye ought to behold."

    " You too involved?" cried Ida, raising
her hands to heaven.

    " Yes, I too. I am suspected of hav-
" ing procured your admittance. There
" are yet no proofs against me, but, as
" they wish to get rid of a person, already
" blackened by suspicion, they are busily
" inquiring into things, which . . . ." I can-

not wholly deny, Walter would have said, but a sorrowful shrug of the shoulders, supplied the deficiency of the sentence.

The reader may perhaps have observed, that Walter had not always the art of framing his answers suitable to the inviolable reserve of a free judge. He had more than once infringed on the duty imposed on him by the title, in favour of Munster, of Ida, and perhaps even of Herman. It could be proved too, that he was the steward of Conrad of Langen, condemned by the secret tribunal, and there were strong presumptions, that his oblique hints had furnished Conrad with the means of so frequently escaping its vengeance. This indeed, was his true crime; the adventure of Ida being only a pretext employed in order to lead to its discovery. But the princess, as if she had not sorrow enough of her own, understood what he had said in its literal sense, and considering herself as the sole cause of the misfortune that threatened him,

L 4

she became thereby plunged still deeper in
the abyss of misery. She forgot the motive
of Walter's visit; she forgot to ask what
means she was to take for her safety; and
remained in a state of absolute insensibility
till the next day, when a visit from duke
Albert restored to her her feelings.

The noble duke of Austria had frequently visited the princess since the absence of count Everard. He had always
esteemed her; and Herman might have
saved himself the trouble of requesting the
duke to watch over her and not leave her
to her fate, as he felt himself voluntarily
disposed to it.

Ida had already bestowed her confidence
on the friend of her lover. To discover
the cause of her new unhappiness, he had
only to ask the question, which he did, and
was immediately informed of what had
passed the preceding night.

Though duke Albert was not affiliated
to the secret tribunal, he knew enough on
the subject to console her. He had before

calmed in a manner her apprehensions respecting her father's fate, and he now attempted the same respecting that of honest Walter, to whom she owed too many obligations not to be interested in it.

" As to the count of Wirtemberg, I " have already observed," said he, " that " the place he holds in the society of the " invisibles, is probably too elevated for " him to have any thing to fear from his " brethren, on a simple suspicion, farther " than a temporary deposition from his dig- " nities, and orders to retire to some place " of secrecy, as well from regard to appear- " ances, as to inspire the inferior mem- " bers of the tribunal with wholesome fear, " and induce them to discharge with punc- " tuality the duties of their oath. This in- " deed, at the present moment, cannot " but be extremely disagreeable to your fa- " ther, as it obliges him to quit the assem- " bly of competitors for the imperial crown " before the accomplishment of his grand " design : but there is no reason to enter-

L 5

" tain any apprehensions for his life.—
" And as to Walter, it is much easier for a
" subaltern to escape, than a judge of
" distinction; and his only punishment
" will probably consist in being deprived
" of his office, a deprivation that I can
" easily repair by my protection and boun-
" ty."

It was absolutely necessary that Albert
should begin with removing the fears of the
princess respecting those whom she had reduced to difficulties and dangers, if he
would rouse her attention, and point it to
herself.   For how could he ever have prevailed on her to seek her own safety, while
so strongly alarmed for that of others?

Having thus paved the way, he entered
on what he conceived to be the most important subject.   He pointed out to the
princess the peril to which she was exposed,
and endeavoured to convince her that it was
not so slight as she imagined.   " Reflect,"
said he, " reflect once more on the words of
" Walter: ' *Both the present and the past will be*

" *examined anew.*' Probably you will not be
" brought to account solely for . . . . what
" shall I call it? . . . . your imprudent
" dream. Your innocence on a former oc-
" casion was acknowledged only in conse-
" quence of the oath of the count of Wir-
" temberg, and as he is divested of his dig-
" nities, the oath is now perhaps annulled,
" so that you may be exposed afresh to the
" malice of your enemies. How many
" things may happen before your father is
" in a situation to come to your succour!
" Who knows whether secret plans be not
" already forming to entrap you? Who
" knows whether, like Herman, you are not
" condemned to be put to death secretly
" and without warning?"

In this manner did the good Albert continue to talk to the young princess till he
succeeded in convincing her of the necessity of flight. She even resolved not to de-
fer it for a day, and to chuse for her retreat whatever place he should recommend;
giving him however to understand, that, as

to the latter point, she believed she had a plan better than any thing he could pro‑pose.

Albert smiled, and asked where she wished to direct her steps?

" It is not a duty incumbent on me," said she, " to repair, in her present misfor‑ " tune, to my friend Sophia, and prove to " her that, formerly, when surrounded with " all the splendor of a throne, she did not " bestow her favour on one capable of in‑ " gratitude?"

" The sentiment," replied the duke, " does honour to your heart : but consider " princess, that your object is to remain " concealed, and that this is impossible in " a place in which the depraved Winces‑ " laus resides."

" Well then," said Ida, " I have a se‑ " cond plan that is not liable to this objec‑ " tion. The peaceful habitation in which " I was educated at Prague will be an " asylum perfectly secure. I will visit him " whom I once called my father, her who

" acted to me as a mother; I will again
" become the humble Ida Munster, and I
" shall then once more be happy. '

" And will it not be there that your
" pursuers will first diret their search after
" you? The idea of retiring to a place
" where you spent the happiest days of
" your life,, is so natural, that, believe me,
" princess, it will occur to them as well as
" to you."

" Alas! where then am I to go; Whi-
" ther, whither am I to wander? Is there
" on earth no safety for persecuted inno-
" cence?"

" Yes, I will tell you where you may
" be safe. There is a young lady, a wor-
" thy and amiable creature to whom I
" have been betrothed from my infancy.
" My love for her could alone enable me
" to converse with the charming princess of
" Wirtemberg in the unimpassioned lan-
" guage of friendship. It is the daughter
" of Sigismond by his former queen Mary.
" She lives in Hungary, in the retirement

" of a convent, situated in the depth of a
" forest amidst the Carpathian mountains.
" Thither I wish you to be conducted. She
" will love you as a sister; no one will
" suspect your retreat; and if by chance it
" should be discovered, the sanctity of the
" place, and the respect due to her whose
" friend you will become, will be your pro-
" tection.   O Ida, if you knew my Eliza-
" beth, you would think her worthy of your
" confidence.   She is yet young, but early
" misfortune has rendered her wise.   She
" possesses not perhaps all the personal
" beauty of the princess of Wirtemberg;
" but her mind! her angelic mind! . . . .
" is the counterpart of your own!"

The emotion of duke Albert, as he pronounced these words, was visible.   He rose
hastily, pressed the hand of Ida, and quitted the apartment.

The heart of our heroine was not less
moved   She was penetrated with the liveliest gratitude towards her friend, though
there was something in his manner which

made her not sorry for his departure.—
Meanwhile she thought too modestly of her
own charms, she had too good an opinion
of the constancy of a knight like Albert, to
fear his failing, on her account, in his fidelity to Elizabeth. No; that appeared to
her as impossible as for herself to forget her
beloved Herman.

The good genius however, which ever
accompanies innocence, whispered notwithstanding frequently in her ear, and
particularly on this occasion, that Albert's
attentions to her were too lively, too tender, and . . . . that flight was the best measure she could take.

In the afternoon he returned. " Prin-
" cess," said he, " I interpreted your si-
" lence this morning into consent. Ac-
" cordingly every thing is ready for your
" journey; you may depart this very night.
" In the mean time, permit me, till the
" hour arrives, to bear you company. It
" would be painful to me to leave you, and
" I have besides things of importance to

" communicate, which I could wish my
" Elizabeth to learn from your mouth.—
" You will perhaps be the means of ren-
" dering us happier than we had hopes of
" being, and of our finding a mother
" whom, alas! we have long supposed
" dead; but who, I have lately been given
" to understand by Herman, is still alive."

The confidence which duke Albert re-
posed in the princess of Wirtemberg claim-
ed of itself some attention, and the manner in which he expressed himself interested
her still more.   She lost therefore not a
syllable of the project which, during the
few hours they spent together, he imparted
to her.   She already knew from Herman
that the countess of Cyly had declared
queen Mary to be living; but she now first
heard where this unfortunate queen resided, and by what means it was intended
to draw her from her obscurity, and restore
her to the place which belonged to her, now
occupied by the worthless Barbe.

The project of Albert appeared vast and difficult of accomplishment to the princess of Wirtemberg; but she promised punctually to observe the directions he gave her; and, having taken leave of him, she at length set off on her journey, which was prolonged more than half by the precautions she thought herself obliged to take to prevent being surprised.

CHAPTER XVIII.

HERMAN's journey was shorter and less hazardous. To avoid the snares that might be laid for him, he generally travelled by night, and had disguised himself so as not to be known. Thus he arrived without the smallest accident in the territories of the old count of Unna. Eager to recover the inprescriptible rights of man, namely, security and the liberty of appearing with undisguised and open countenance among his brethren of mankind, he delayed not a moment the visit he purposed to make to a person, who, according to duke Albert, was able to restore him to the enjoyment of those blessings.— Divesting himself therefore of every unfavourable prejudice towards his relation, that had been instilled into his infant mind, and endeavouring to recollect all that would awaken confidence, he no sooner arrived than he demanded audience of the old count for a stranger, commissioned by duke Albert of Austria to impart to him an affair of the greatest importance.

The count of Unna was absent. Some new disputes that had arisen between the count of Tecklenburg and the bishop of Munster, in which he was chosen arbiter, had called him some weeks from home, and Herman was obliged to wait with patience his return. Accordingly he had sufficient leisure to reflect on the singularity of his situation. He found himself in his native country; he saw around him a hundred places he had known when a child. Mixed ideas, pleasing and unpleasing, were recalled to his mind. The sole motive of his visit to this district was to ask succour of a man against whom he had imbibed prejudices that he could not yet entirely surmount. In the neighbourhood lived his brothers and sisters with whom his infancy had been spent, but on whom, in his present difficulty, he dared not confide.

The reader will recollect, that, at the age of twelve or thirteen years, Herman had fled from the terrors of a convent, in which he was on the point of being immured, to become one of the pages of the emperor Winceslaus. So libertine a step could not fail to displease his relations, most of whom, male as well as female, had embraced a monastic life; accordingly they had since held little correspondence with the graceless fugitive.

Herman had been at first too happy, and afterwards too much occupied by his various adventures to concern himself much about his family. He had had little communication with any of them, except his sisters, Agnes and Petronilla, once the loved companions of his tender years, but who since, sacrificed to the interest of their elder brother, had taken the veil in the convent of Uberwasser.

The art of letter-writing was then not much in use, and few attended to it so little as those decorated with the order of knighthood. We may presume, therefore, that Herman was no very punctual correspondent. Yet our manuscript informs us, that no important event happened to him, with which he did not acquaint the nuns of Uberwasser; and that he received no present, however small, in which Agnes and Petronilla did not share.

I will not enquire, whether these nuns were always so prudent as not to betray the confidence he placed in them: but certain it is, that his elder brothers and sisters were acquainted with all the leading occurrences of his life. From these Herman received on different occasions, some very extraordinary letters. At one time his brother, the canon of Munster, at another his sister, the abbess of Marienhagen, wrote to tell him their sentiments, at such a distance, of things that passed in a world with which they were totally unacquainted.

. The remonstrances with which these letters were filled, had never been well re-

ceived by our mettlesome youth; and he
had uniformly been so unpolite as to leave
them unanswered; a circumstance from
which he had reason to presume that the
regard these personages of his family formerly entertained for him must be totally
extinguished, and their displeasure, on account of his escape to the court of Winceslaus, considerably augmented.

These therefore were not the relations,
that, on his arrival in his native soil, he was
desirous of seeing. But he felt differently
respecting another brother, destined like
himself for a cloister, and his sisters Agnes
and Petronilla, with whom he frequently
wished to beguile the hours, while he solita-
rily waited the return of the old count of
Unna. At length he ventured to enquire
after them, and was informed that his brother John had quitted the convent to enter
into the teutonic order of knights, but that
the nuns of Uberwasser were still in their
monastery.

The count's stay being protracted, and Herman finding himself perfectly in the midst of strangers, he resolved to visit the monastery. He wanted some friendly bosom into which he might pour the overflowings of his heart.

He presented himself and was admitted to the grate of the parlour. Agnes and Petronilla were there, but they were not alone. His heart was on the wing to meet them; but the presence of a third person was a restraint on him, and induced him to withhold the effusions of brotherly affection till she should withdraw.

The stranger, whose countenance could boast no great expression, kept her eyes intently fixed on him, and seemed so anxious to discover his name, by endeavouring to recollect his features, that, for a while, she addressed not a word to the nuns, whom she was just come to see.

Herman, extremely agitated, was equally silent.

"I perceive you can dispense with my presence," said the lady at last to the nuns, at the same time rising from her chair. " The knight, I presume, is not come merely to look at you: or are you such adepts in the language of the eyes, that you can understand what he would say, without its being necessary for him to open his mouth?"

" We have not the honour of knowing the gentleman," answered Agnes, " though there is certainly something in his features . . . ."

" That very much pleases you:" added the lady with a sneer. " A pretty frank confession for a couple of nuns, I must own."

" I appeal to yourself, sir knight," said Agnes in a tone of some displeasure, " Say, are you at all known to us?"

" Agnes and Petronilla then do not know me? And have they no presentiment?" replied Herman, with a smile of tenderness.

"Come, explain yourselves, young ladies," said the visitor, who, by degrees,
as she fancied she recollected Herman,
viewed him with eyes still more unfavourable: "You ought to have some presenti-
"ment; the knight himself acknowledges
"it."

"Ah! if suspicions, if presentiments
"were to determine," answered Petronilla,
"it is so long since I heard from my bro-
"ther Herman, I should say you came
"from him."

"*My* brother, indeed!" cried the lady
with petulance. "Are you then the only
"sister of the little urchin? But your
"brothers and sisters will have no great
"objection to relinquish to you the ho-
"nour."

"And who is this little urchin of whom
"you speak?" Asked the knight, giving
her a look of contempt.

"Pray, sir, pardon her!" said the
gentle Agnes. "We frequently give this
"appellation to those whom we have seen

" when children. I suspect that you are
" the friend of our Herman; and I trust
" you will not be offended at what has been
" said. The lady is . . . ."

" None of your excuses, Miss," said
the lady interrupting her: " None of your
" excuses for me. I shall not so far de-
" grade myself as to make any either to
" Herman or any of his friends. And as
" to pardon, it is he I think who stands
" most in need of that. His scandalous
" return to the world, and the total forget-
" fulness of his relations and benefactors,
" are not yet effaced from our memory:
" nor is the life he has since led at all cal-
" culated to remove these unfavourable im-
" pressions."

" Fie, Catherine!" said Petronilla in
a suppliant rather than a reproving tone.
" What harm has Herman done you that
" you should thus speak ill of him before
" a stranger?"

" Before a stranger! Did you not say,
" that you supposed him to be the friend

" and envoy of your brother? Be this how-
" ever as it may, every body knows his
" shameful adventures with the paltry little
" Munster, who, God knows how, is on a
" sudden become a princess; the share he
" had in the murder of the duke of Bruns-
" wic; and a variety of other crimes that
" have occasioned him to be condemned
" by the secret tribunal, and that ought
" for ever to alienate the heart of his re-
" lations." Saying this, she rose, and
flounced out of the parlour, while Herman, with arms folded, looked at her with
horror.

" May I ask," said Herman, when she
was gone, " who this fury is?"

" Our sister, Catherine of Senden," replied Petronilla with a sigh.

" Your sister! Your sister! Good Hea-
" vens can it be! And if yours, conse-
" quently mine! Alas, alas!"

" Who then are you?" cried Agnes, ad-
vancing nearer the grate in order to observe him more distinctly.

M 2

"O Herman, Herman!" exclaimed Petronilla, clasping her hands. "Yes it is "indeed our Herman! My heart did not "deceive me."

"My brother! My good angel! Our "only comfort under all our afflictions!" said Agnes weeping. Ah! why cannot I fold thee in my arms!"

The rapture of these kind and virtuous souls at sight of a brother whom they fondly loved, and from whom they had so long been separated, is not to be described, and for a while it bereft Herman of the power of speech .... At length their joy becoming more calm, he again spoke of her who had made on him so unfavourable an impression, who had so furiously reviled, and strove with so much malice to dishonour him. He was astonished that such a woman could be his sister, and the nuns were obliged to give him a thousand different proofs before they could convince him.

"Good God!" cried he, "and are "the rest of the family like her? If so, I "will never make myself known to any "but yourselves."

"Judge not so hastily," said the good Agnes. "Catherine is unhappy. Mis- "fortune frequently renders us unjust, and "we ought to make allowance for those "who are the butt of its shafts, whatever "reason we may have to complain of "them."

This reflection softened Herman. He asked farther questions. "You know," said Petronilla, "that she was preparing "for a religious life when we took the "veil; but she preferred an indifferent "match, and now suffers from the poverty "and neglect of her husband and the re- "proaches of her elder brothers and "sisters, particularly the abbess of Marien- "hagen. Ill treated, as she conceives, "by them, she is disposed to take her "revenge on others: but she would pro- "bably not have displayed her ill-humour

M 3

" in the manner she has just done, had not
" her dissatisfaction been excited the mo-
" ment before you came in by a conversa-
" tion respecting you."

" Respecting me !"

" Yes, respecting you, my dear bro-
" ther.   But, Heavens ! can it be true ?
" Is it possible that you are pursued by the
" secret tribunal?"

" Be not uneasy, my dear sister, on that
" account.   Supposing it true, God is the
" safeguard and protector of innocence."

The nuns began to weep, and it was difficult for Herman so far to tranquilize their
feelings as to obtain from them the information he wanted.

" Picture to yourself our despair when
" we heard the dreadful intelligence.   Ag-
" nes expressed a wish, that you might take.
" refuge in your own country.; a wish in
" which I sincerely joined, hoping that you
" would find an asylum with our brother
" Bernard, or at least assistance to enable
" you to seek your safety elsewhere, for we

" had no doubt of your poverty. And
" where, added I, can he apply with
" greater confidence than to the head of
" his family, his own brother, who ought
" to act the part of a father to him? Ca-
" therine at this became enraged. She
" has a numerous family, and she con-
" ceived that whatever Bernard might give
" you would be taken from her children,
" who, she hopes, will one day inherit the
" whole of his fortune."

Herman directed towards his sisters a
look, that expressed his gratitude, and the
regret he felt at not being able to testify it
as he could wish. The sorrow he displayed
in his countenance was misinterpreted.—
" Do not afflict yourself, my dear brother,"
said Agnes with emotion, holding out to
him her hand. " If Bernard refuses, we
" will assist you ourselves; we are not so
" poor as you may imagine; all the pre-
" sents we have received from you are still
" in our possession; and will perhaps prove
" sufficient. But ah! whither will you go?

M 4

"Where can you be safe from your
"avengers? Petronilla, do you advise him;
"you are generally fertile in expedients:
"but be quick; a moment's delay may be
"ruinous."

Herman had no means of quieting the
apprehensions of his sisters, but by a relation of his adventures, from which they
saw that the danger, at least as he flattered
himself, was not so imminent as they had
been told, that he had wherewith to provide for his support, and that discretion
was all that was necessary to his safety.

Our party was in no haste to separate.
The rules of the convent were not very
rigid, and our nuns besides were so extremely beloved that they might remain in
the parlour as long as they pleased. The
conversation however, which had lasted
some hours, was at length interrupted by
the arrival of the abbess of Marienhagen,
who came to visit her sisters, and acquaint
them with the reports that were spread concerning Herman.

She recollected him the moment she entered, and was as readily recollected by
him. Nuns, they say, have a quicker sight
and stronger memory than your profane
worldlings. It was impossible for our knight
to conceal himself from the abbess: nor
did it become him, he thought, to show
distrust of a sister whom, in his infancy, he
had been taught to revere as a mother.

Ursula embraced him. Her kiss was
cold, yet was it preferable to the conduct
of madam Senden. She presently related,
in pious and measured phrases, nearly the
same things which Catherine had mentioned
with acrimony and passion. He perceived
that at bottom neither of them loved him:
but while the rage of madam Senden excited his indignation, the behaviour of the
abbess was entitled to some respect, and he
resolved to relate to her his adventures, in
order to disprove the injurious reports propagated concerning him.

Ursula, having heard his story, shrugged up her shoulders, and expressed a hope

M 5

that it might be true: but he had better,
she said, have sought his safety in some
other country, as it was impossible to find
an asylum among his relations ; and that
the utmost they could do for him was to
favour his flight.

Sentiments so unnatural revolted the
mind of Herman. He was silent and fell
into a profound reverie. Meanwhile Petronilla related to the abbess the discourse
of Catherine, which kindled the holy ma-
tron into a flame.

" I penetrate her designs," cried Ursula.
" The moment she is sure of the arrival of
" Herman, she will exert herself to pre-
" vent the lord of Unna," [such was the
respectful title under which Bernard was
always spoken of by his sisters] " from
" having an interview with him, lest he
" should be induced to do something for
" his distressed brother. But she shall not
" succeed in her plan : and though flight
" is certainly the most advisable step for
" Herman, yet I see no reason why he

" may not stay a few days and be intro-
" duced to his relations, as he has certainly
" as much right to the assistance of his bro-
" ther as the selfish Catherine."

Herman trembled at the enmity Ursula
displayed for her sister, though at the same
time she was testifying her goodness towards him. He assured her that he was not
come to ask assistance, or to remain many
days losing the time which was of importance to his flight; that he wished not to give
umbrage to any one by his presence; and
that he had undertaken this journey by the
advice of the duke of Auftria, who had led
him to hope, that the old count of Unna,
chief of the secret tribunal in those parts,
could effect a farther investigation of his
unhappy affair, and procure him an opportunity of proving his innocence.

The name of the count of Unna was to
the abbess of Marienhagen as an electrical
shock. She vowed that she would never
suffer a brother whom she had brought up
and always loved as her own child, to claim

the protection of the declared enemy of her
family. All their ancient feuds, which Herman had been obliged so often to hear repeated as to be sick with disgust, were now
recited anew. She told him how the old
count of Unna had, both publicly and pri-
vately, persecuted the lords of Unna on
account of the affair of Wirtemberg; how
he had seized their property, and obliged
the greater part of them, herself among
the rest, to embrace a religious life for
want of means to support with proper dignity the rank to which they were born;
how he continued still to hate and despise
them to such a degree, that he was resolved,
as he had no children, rather than leave to
them his earldom of Unna, with its do-
mains, to bequeath them to some foreign
house, or suffer them to devolve on the
emperor.

Herman was satiated with the verbose
prolixity of this narration. He attempted
to reply, but the abbess would not listen to
him, and made him consent to be intro-

duced the next day to his elder brother, who resided at Plettenburg.

It grew late, and Herman was obliged to quit the sisters he loved, together with her towards whom he felt no partiality. At his departure Ursula embraced him more tenderly than at first, and she obtained permission for the door of the parlour to be opened that Agnes and Petronilla might have the same pleasure: marks of benevolence that would have touched the susceptible heart of our chevalier, had he not been aware that the desire of giving pain to others was their true motive.

CHAPTER XIX.

HOW much must Herman have regretted the agreeable society of the duke of Austria, the interesting Ida, and the worthy Munster, on comparing it with that of some of his relations, whose way of thinking was to him equally new and disgusting. It is true, that it fell short of the extreme depravity he had observed in a few other persons, as Kunzman, and the countess of Cyly, for instance : but the meanness of their souls inspired him with a certain antipathy, which never fails to be accompanied with contempt; though the feeling was in a manner softened by his reflecting on the amiable nuns of Uberwasser. Indeed his desire of seeing these once more, had greater weight in prolonging his stay, than the promise he had made to the abbess of Marienhagen: for he feared he might find other disagreeable originals in his family, and should at last be obliged to suspect his own goodness, the branches of the tree from which he descended being so corrupt.

The so much dreaded day at length arrived, and he set off for Marienhagen, where he had promised to call for his sister, the abbess. With her he found the whole family assembled, except the important personage to whom he was to be introduced. Agnes and Petronilla ran with open arms to meet him. The phlegmatic canoness of Munster, coldly held out to him her hand, and madam Senden, by the positive order of the devout Ursula, stammered her excuses. Herman had long before pardoned her, and he was sorry he had been offended with her for a single moment; the deep humiliation impressed on her countenance gave him pain, and he embraced her with warmth, calling her by the tender name of sister.

By her side was her husband, Ulric of Senden, whose figure was one of those, which nature rarely forms, displaying that model of human beauty in its utmost per-

fection, which the Grecian artist imagined
for his Apollo, while the expression of his
features bespoke a mind not at all inferior.
He embraced our knight with dignity; and
Herman, won, as is usual with young persons, by the impression of external charms,
pressed him with ardour to his bosom. He
was suprised at finding a physiognomy of
this description, in a circle of persons, the
majority of whom had little to boast in point
of beauty, and still more, that such a man
should be the husband of Catherine; and he
looked at the two nuns to express to them
his astonishment. They smiled and whispered to him to prepare himself to see, in
another relation, a person far surpassing all
his imagination could conceive.

At length the cavalcade set out for Plettenburg. Ulric appeared as much dissatisfied as Herman, with the attention so numerous a company would excite, and had a
serious conversation with the abbess on the
subject, to whom he observed, that such
parade was by no means prudent, consi-

dering the situation of the young stranger. But his remonstrances were useless. No one would dare to talk openly of the danger of Herman, now that the devout abbess of Marienhagen treated him with kindness, and had taken him under her protection ; and the reports of his misfortune were to be blotted from remembrance, the moment she issued the injunction, though before, no one had propagated it with so much imprudence as herself, and Catherine, whom she hated, though so strongly resembling her.

Herman had resided at the courts of the first princes of his time; he had been in the service of an emperor, and of a king of Hungary; at Nuremberg he had been familiar with personages who had pretensions to the first throne in the world; yet had he no where witnessed that ostentatious display of grandeur, which obtruded itself on the eye, at the castle of a mere country gentleman.

'Bernard must surely have thought, that the honour of being chief of the younger branch of the house of Unna, was the most exalted to which human vanity could aspire, or he could never have endured the ridiculous pomp that surrounded him; could never have been pleased with the humble homage of his relations and domestics; could never have treated, with such haughtiness, all who approached him.

The court of Plettenburg, as Bernard's residence was then styled, was certainly too splendid for a lord of Unna; but it was a splendor by which Herman, who had seen the world, was not to be dazzled, and which could not fail to excite, in a philosophic mind, the most melancholy reflections. All this magnificence was supported by the un-paid dowries of unhappy sisters, and the with-holden fortunes of brothers scarcely more happy, who had sacrificed themselves, or been forcibly sacrificed, to enable the first born of the family to live in the style of a petty sovereign.

Displeasing as was to Herman the house which he entered; its master, though his brother, proved equally displeasing. The audience he obtained was by no means favourable. He ought, if he would conform to established rules, to have bowed himself as lowly in the presence of Bernard, as before king Sigismond, or the emperor Winceslaus. This he avoided, accosting him only with the respect which he conceived due to an elder brother; but he soon perceived the dissatisfaction occasioned by this conduct, which was deemed irreverent.

The eyes of Herman were soon attracted from this haughty gentleman, to a young woman seated by his side, who, as soon as the abbess had announced the name of the chevalier, rose with inimitable grace to embrace him. It was the wife of Bernard. She was unknown to Herman, as she had not been united to the family till after his his elopement.

He looked at her with astonishment. His Ida excepted, he had never beheld so perfect a beauty. Her charms were heightened by angelic sweetness, spread over every feature of her face, and forming a perfect contrast to the stiff and formal demeanour of her imperious spouse; as well as by a trait of melancholy, an interesting paleness, that plainly bespoke her to be unhappy, and which, to the eye of sensibility, is irresistibly attracting.

Alicia took the hand of Herman, and called him a second time her brother, and that in a tone so endearing that the heart of our knight was inexpressibly moved, and he could not refrain from falling at her feet.

Bernard beheld with satisfaction this mark of respect, which he supposed was paid rather to the consort of the lord of Unna, than to the beautiful Alicia. Imagining therefore that Herman did not altogether disdain the etiquette of his court, he held out his hand, with a tolerable grace, to assist him to rise. That of his charming sister-in-law Herman presumed to kiss, and having seated himself in a chair by her side, which was negligently offered him by Bernard, he was honoured with a few questions, which he took care to answer so as not to offend the pride of his brother.

Shortly after, the lord of Unna being engaged in a private conversation with his sister, the abbess, Alicia, made a sign to the nuns of Uberwasser, her intimate and bosom friends, to approach, in order to converse with Herman.

"Well, my dear brother," said Petronilla with a smile, " is our prediction " verified?"

" Oh!" replied Herman, " I am asto- " nished, enchanted! I could fancy my- " self in the company of my beloved Ida, " and I esteem myself happy in having so " lovely a sister."

Alicia was about to make a civil reply to this compliment, but, having cast her eye on Ulric of Senden, who was leaning against a pillar opposite to her, and who seemed as in a trance with the pleasure of beholding her, she blushed, and was silent.

The mind of Herman was too busily occupied to notice her embarrassment.— Every thing surprised him; and a whole day spent in his brother's house served only to convince him that he was far from being acquainted with the history of all the individuals of his family.

That of Ulric of Senden he was least able to decypher. His figure, his manner, were extremely prepossessing; yet, in his behaviour to Herman, was there something singularly forbidding. Grave and cold when he talked to him; and, at the same time, when he spoke of him to a third person, his ardent admirer. All the efforts of our young chevalier to induce Ulric to unite himself to him by the ties of friendship were vain; on the contrary he appeared to shun every opportunity of entering into private conversation with Herman, and smiled on him only when he saw him in the midst of a numerous circle.—

His behaviour to madam Unna was equally strange. If he found himself obliged to speak to her, it was in a tone of indifference bordering on contempt; yet were his eyes, when he thought himself unobserved, incessantly fixed on her. He carefully avoided meeting her, yet could not refrain from watching her every motion, listening to her every word.

.Having observed all this, it appeared by no means extraordinary to Herman, that so singular a character should express no great tenderness to Catherine; but he was at a loss to conceive how she could have become his wife. To clear his doubts he had recourse to the nuns, his sisters; who shrugged their shoulders, and assured him that they were not sufficiently acquainted with the affair to give him the information he wished.

Madam Unna displayed a great predilection for her new brother-in-law. He and his two sisters, Agnes and Petronilla, formed her select society. Never did she

so much strive to engage him to herself
as when she perceived him making attempts
to gain the friendship of Ulric, who could
with difficulty preserve the cool air he assumed towards him. " Why," said she to
him one day, " are you always courting the
" friendship of that singular being? I must
" insist on your promising me never to
" contract any intimacy with him: he is
" honest enough to reject your overtures,
" and I dare affirm he has reasons for it."

Herman seized this opportunity of putting some questions to Alicia respecting
Ulric; but, instead of answering them, she
blushed, and endeavoured to give another
turn to the conversation.

CHAPTER XX.

THE different members of the family of Unna remained at the castle of Plettenburg for some days. Bernard seemed insensibly to take a liking to Herman. The young chevalier could relate so many anecdotes of kings and emperors, of dukes and princes, that the haughty loid began to feel some veneration for him, and to excuse his not having humbled himself more before the head of his house; he was also inwardly flattered by the profound respect paid by Herman to the beautiful Alicia.

At length the abbess of Marienhagen, and the nuns of Uberwasser were obliged to return to their respective convents.— The unwieldy canoness of Munster also quitted the castle, so that of Bernard's guests none remained but Herman and the family of Senden.

N

Catherine availed herself of the absence of the abbess, her mortal enemy, to show herself to the brother, whom at first she had so highly offended, in a more favourable point of view. She perceived that his endeavours to obtain the friendship of Bernard were perfectly disinterested ; some considerable presents which he made her children, proved also that he neither sought nor needed assistance; and this was sufficient to inspire her with regret for having given him so ill a reception.— She made him therefore many advances, and one day said, that she should never think he had forgiven her, unless he would promise to accompany her home, and thus afford her an opportunity of repairing the injury.

Herman had nothing so much at heart as to attain an audience of the old count of Unna, who, he had heard, was returned. It was the sole business that had brought him into this country; the visits he had paid his family were merely casual, and had already occupied more time than was prudent in his situation. He would therefore unquestionably have refused madam Senden's request, in which her husband had no part, had he not feared that she might think he still harboured resentment in his breast for the manner in which she had treated him. He accordingly consented, a step which occasioned madam Unna, who was present, a degree of uneasiness which she could with difficulty conceal.

" Is then every entreaty I have made " you, not to contract an intimacy with " Ulric of Senden, useless?" said she to him the moment they were alone.

" It is not Ulric that I am going to visit; " it is my sister."

" But when you are in his house, will " you be able to prevent a certain degree " of familiarity from taking place between " you?"

" And would not the friendship of such " a man be a happiness to me?"

N 2

. " I tell you no, Herman, no. You
" must never be alone with him for a single
" moment; if you are, some calamity will
" befal you."

" I do not comprehend you, madam.—
" Would you have me entertain suspicions
" injurious to the honour of Ulric?"

" Certainly not. Ulric may be a man
" of the nicest honour; but . . . . I dare
" not be more explicit . . . . Believe me,
" Herman, the most prudent step you can
" take is to repair with all speed to the old
" count of Unna, to finish your business
" with him, and then to depart."

" I have nothing madam, nearer at
" heart, than to see the count of Unna; but
" I cannot dispense with visiting my sister;
" it would be cruel to treat her with un-
" kindness."

" I have no hatred to Catherine; I pity
" her, and ascribe many of her faults to the
" unpleasantness of her situation."

" And yet you give me to understand,
" that I have something to apprehend from

" her which ought to deter me from enter-
" ing her house."

" Not from her. God forbid! not from
" her. I do not think her wicked enough
" secretly to injure you . . . . But Ulric of
" Senden! Ulric!"

" Is a worthy and virtuous character:
" is to our sex, what the divine Alicia is to
" hers!"

"" He may be virtuous, he may be wor-
" thy; and yet . . . . have I not known
" him longer than you?"

" Certainly, certainly, you are best ac-
" quainted with him. I have observed
" your looks; I have observed his also; I
" have noticed things that make me wish
" to know more . . . . Alicia, frank and
" amiable Alicia! my sister, my friend!
" will you not trust me? My advice may
" possibly be of service to you. Possibly,
" by telling me your real sentiments of
" Ulric I may be induced to embrace your
" counsel. Will you then not listen to my

N 3

" prayer? Say, will you not condescend to
" explain yourself?

Alicia shed a torrent of tears; but disengaging herself from Herman, who held
her hands in his, she declared that she
would have no farther conversation with
him on the subject. " Remember how-
" ever," added she, " remember that I
" have warned you. You must now act
" as you please. I have nothing more to
" say."

She appeared seriously offended with
our chevalier for his too urgent importunities, and would not address a single word to
him during the remainder of the day, the
last he was to spend at her house. Meanwhile she had yet not abandoned the hope
of separating him from Ulric.

Herman persisted in his intention of ac-
companying his sister home, and as soon as
it was known, Ulric was invited to stay a
few days longer at Plettenburg.

A deadly paleness overspread the countenance of Ulric, the moment our young

man informed him that he purposed to pay
him a visit; but, upon receiving this invitation from Bernard and Alicia, his cheeks
again resumed their wonted animation.——
Herman observed, for the first time, that
he kissed the hand of his sister-in-law, and
spoke to her with politeness. Alicia
blushed, and cast down her eyes, while Ulric fixed on her a look of the liveliest gratitude.

"What means this change?" said Herman to himself. "Am I deceived respect-
"ing these two characters? Are they less
"scrupulous, less delicate than I had ima-
"gined? .... Ah! they are certainly en-
"gaged in a secret, a guilty commerce.——
"Their stolen looks, their sudden blushes,
"their mutual intelligence attest that they
"have formerly loved, and that their love
"is yet not extinguished .... Was it for
"this, dissembling Alicia, thou soughtest
"to separate me from Ulric? No doubt,
"thou wert afraid I should discover thy
"criminal passion, and seek to avenge a

N 4

" brother's injured honour.   No doubt,
" thou wishest to retain him at Plettenburg
" that thou mayest tranquilly enjoy thy
" illicit attachment, free from the eyes of
" a jealous wife, and a suspicious brother-
" in-law."

To Herman appearances pleaded so
strong against Alicia, that he was astonished
at the blindness of Bernard, who seemed
not to remark things, that, in his opinion,
must be perceived by all the world; and
it was, perhaps, happy for the suspected parties that Herman was not eager to communicate to his brother his reflections.

The chevalier departed with Catherine
and her children.   They were handsome
and diverting little creatures, more resembling their father than their mother, and
with them he beguiled the wearisomeness
of his sister's insipid conversation.

He was every instant more convinced of
the depravity of this woman's heart.   Her
slanderous tongue spared not an individual
of her relations, whom she endeavoured to

ruin in the mind of her young brother, not excepting even the innocent nuns of Uberwasser, Agnes and Petronilla. She vaunted, with great self-complacency, the dexterity with which she could discover evil in the inmost recesses of the heart, and adduced proofs of her talent that were really singular in their kind.

She had found means to procure the paper on which madam Unna had written the examination of her conscience, and Herman expected nothing less from this circumstance than a confirmation of his suspicions; but, to his extreme surprise, he found them removed.

"This Alicia," said Catherine, "a poor
" descendant of the house of Langen, be-
" come obnoxious to the secret tribunal,
" has entered into our family to our sorrow.
" But for her, Bernard would probably
" never have thought of marrying. How-
" ever she is faithfully attached to him, and
" is scarcely ever from his side, which
" renders her the plague of all the wives in

N 5

" the neighbourhood, whose hufbands are
" continually citing her as a model.—She
" is not disagreeable in her person, as you
" have seen; neither has she wanted ad-
" mirers; and for a while I could not help
" thinking that she indemnified herself in
" private for the strict decorum she affected
" in public : but having narrowly watched
" her for some years, I am at length convinced
" that she is a woman devoid both of spirit
" and sensibility, to whom such kind of
" virtue costs little."

Herman looked at Catherine with eyes
of astonishment, and would have asked,
but knew not how, the reason of the understanding he observed between Alicia and
Ulric.

" Is she friendly to you and your hus-
" band?" said he at length with an affectation of ind.fference.

" To me she is certainly friendly. You
" see I have a good opinion of her; con-
" sequently I merit her attachment. Be-
" sides, she loves my children, and often

" makes them presents. But for my hus-
" band she appears to entertain the most
" profound contempt. Of this, at least,
" I am certain, that a civil word has never
" passed between them till to-day. You
" were witness to the invitation she gave
" him : it astonished me, for to say the
" truth, he cares as little for her, as she
" for him. He always avoids her, and I
" do not recollect, that, since our marriage,
" he has three times set his foot within the
" doors of Plettenburg castle."

Herman could not avoid shaking his
head, and seeking, by a number of adroit
questions, to discover some traces of what
he suspected. He learnt, however, nothing more, and with pleasure, found himself deceived in the opinion he had formed
of Ulric and Alicia. What better proof indeed could he have had of their innocence,
than the testimony of Catherine? Even in
the enumeration of her complaints against
her husband, she said not a word that could
cast on him the least suspicion of infidelity.

Her griefs all centered in his discontent, and uncivil treatment of her, to which the good lady herself might have given sufficient occasion, by the malignancy of her disposition, of which she had just exhibited no very equivocal proofs.

CHAPTER XXI.

HERMAN had already so amply enjoyed the conversation of his benevolent
sisters on the road, that he was little desirous of renewing it, during his short abode
at her house, and preferred the innocent
prattle of her children, who had easily
gained his affection. He talked to them
continually of their father, and what they
said, exhibited him in so favourable a point
of view, that all his suspicions vanished,
and were succeeded by a new desire of having him for a friend. To this desire was
joined, that of knowing the motive of Alicia's mysterious advice. He determined,
therefore, to have a private interview with
him, and to triumph over the efforts of his
brother-in-law to avoid him.

"My husband,' says Catherine, "seems
" resolved not to return till his presence
" shall be necessary to dissipate the solitude

" in which I live. To speak frankly, I
" scarcely feel the absence of an ill-natured
" spouse, in the company of so agreeable a
" brother. Let him stay, therefore, at Plet-
" tenburg, and strengthen our intimacy
" with Bernard and his wife, which sooner
" or later, may be of advantage to us."
She then shewed Herman a letter she had
just received from Ulric, in which she was
desired to inform him of the departure of
her brother, the instant it took place, as he
should then quit Plettenburg, and return
home.

Herman resolved to be gone the next
day. He accordingly took leave of his
sister and her children, after having given
the latter proofs of his generosity, that deprived him of almost all he possessed. He
knew the road to Unna to be that by which
Ulric must return, and he waited for him
a whole day in the forest through which he
was to pass. The delay shewed, that Ulric
took every possible precaution not to meet,
nor to see him again.

" Heavens!" cried Herman, " what
" can be the cause of this insuperable aver-
" sion? At Plettenburg, I read in his eyes
" the hatred he bore me. The coldness of
" his manner, and the reserve of his con-
" versation, convinced me I was not mista-
" ken. Not once could I prevail upon him
" to take a walk with me. He seemed de-
" voured with chagrin whenever at table,
" or in company, I was accidentally seated
" by his side. Surely, some fearful my-
" stery lurks beneath all this. I must fa-
" thom it. I must give this man, for I
" love him, a better opinion of me, though
" it cost me my life. Perhaps my misfor-
" tune has instilled suspicions into his mind.
" Perhaps he thinks me guilty of the crime
" of which I am accused. Yes, yes, I will
" see him, I will gain his affection, by
" proving to him my innocence. The
" good opinion of the whole world would
" be nothing to me, while Ulric should
" think me capable of murder."

You, who have been sometimes drawn
by an irresistible impulse towards a soul in
unison with your own, without being able
to comprehend the charm that attracted
you; you, whose efforts, to obtain the
good-will of him whom you have chosen
among a thousand, have increased in pro-
portion as the loved object seemed to reject your advances; you alone can judge
of the inclination felt by our chevalier for
Ulric of Senden. The frigid heart which
never experienced this sentiment, would in
vain attempt to form an idea of it.

As evening approached, the anxiety of
Herman increased. The longer he vainly
waited for him whom he wished to see, the
more ardent became his desire. Meanwhile his mind was disturbed; a thousand
melancholy presages crowded to his thoughts;
his heart bad him remain, while a secret
voice whispered to him to fly. " But why
" should I fly?" said he to himself; and he
remained.

The moon arose. Our hero had advanced so far to meet Senden, that he
could perceive, from a hill he had ascended, the turrets of the castle of Plettenburg.
He beheld around him nothing but deserts.
The stillness of the night was interrupted
by no other sound, than the monotonous
murmuring of a brook.

The night was far spent, and the moon
was hastening to the western horizon, when
the sound of horses feet were heard in a nar-
row valley. They drew so near, that Herman could distinguish the voice of Ulric,
directing his servants to go on before to
Senden house, and bring him word, whether the young knight were yet gone. He
then alighted, and seated himself at the foot
of a tree. Herman, who watched his motions, immediately presented himself, and
said to him: " Why dost thou shun me?
" What has Herman done, that it seems
" poison to thee, to breathe the same air
" with him?"

" God of Heaven !" exclaimed Ulric,
wrapping himself in his cloak, " what a
" misfortune! Waking or dreaming he is
" every where present to my sight ; and
" now a voice within me tells me that I
" must kill him."

" That thou must kill me!" said Herman, folding him in his arms : " That thou
" must assassinate thy brother! . . . .
" What, then, what have I done?"

" Begone, villain!" replied Ulric, dis-
" engaging himself from his embrace.——
" Who art thou? . . . . Is it not a vision
" that I see?——Speak, who art thou?"

" Thy brother, Herman of Unna, who
" asks thy friendship or death. To be
" despised, to be rejected by thee, is more
" than he can support."

" Herman? Herman of Unna? . . . .
" Fly, fly! I am thy murderer . . . . Yet
" no, fly not. It is forbidden me to give
" thee such advice; still less can I suffer
" thee to execute it. Are we not alone?
" . . . . No, we are not . . . . God be prais-
" ed! see, where come thy deliverers!"

Herman looked, and saw nothing . . . .
" They are the shadows of the trees, my
" brother. But I need no deliverer when
" thou art with me. O Ulric! Thou art
" ill, very ill! Thy heart is distressed! . . .
" I feared it was hatred that kept thee
" from me; but it was melancholy . . . .
" Heaven be praised! Thy melancholy
" will be dispelled, thy sufferings relieved,
" and thou wilt then love thy brother!"

" Love thee? Can I love thee more
" than I do? O Herman! My heart is
" with thee, and yet must I assassinate
" thee."

" Why:" cried Herman, whom Ulric
for a moment closely pressed in his arms,
and then as rudely repulsed: " Why assassi-
" nate me? What is my crime?"

" Thou must die," replied Senden draw-
ing his sabre: " Thou art the murderer
" of duke Frederic."

" I swear by him, to whom all things
" are known, that I am not."

" The charge has been made, the wit-
" nesses have deposed, and the judges
" have pronounced thy condemnation.—
" Thou art, thou must be the murderer of
" the duke. Thousands of secret execu-
" tioners burn with the desire of shedding
" thy blood: but, O Heavens! Fate has de-
" creed that the task shall devolve on thy
" unfortunate brother. I have bound my-
" self by an oath, an oath the most terrible,
" not to spare those whom the secret tribu-
" nal shall condemn . . . . This then to
" thy heart . . . . This to my own!"

They staggered; they fell side by side.
" Oh my brother," said Herman embrac-
ing Ulric, " the thread of my life is at an
" end. Yet I will be thine, I will ever be
" thine, in those realms above, the abode of
" peace and everlasting friendship."

END OF THE SECOND VOLUME.